FRACTURED

LESLIE DEAN DRURY

This book is a work of fiction. Names, characters, places, and events are either products of the author's imagination or are used fictitiously. Any resemblance to actual events, locales, or persons, living or dead, is entirely coincidental.

Illustrations Â© 2012 Jupiterimages Corporation

www.RasaPublishing.com

ISBN: 978-1-939343-00-0
ISBN: 978-1-939343-01-07 (eBook)

Manufactured in the United States of America

To my grandmother, Sophia Ailcy Combs Caudill,
a profoundly, brave writer of her time.
May we all write with our hearts, just as she did.

To the little girl inside of me, who has never left my side,
though I left hers.
I am back.
I am holding your hand, never again to let go.

Designing with the Fractures: Co-Creation

CHAPTER 1

I t was 3:00 a.m., witching hour.
   On a late September, Indian Summer night.

In silent fury, sixteen year old Sonoma climbed the ancient cobblestone fence behind Café Piraza, the orphanage in Argentina which had housed Sonoma since birth.

Sonoma's feet were bare. Her head shaved. Sonoma's long blonde locks had been severed that morning, another punishment by the school.

Dried blood covered Sonoma's white nightgown. Nine hours had passed since the bloodbath. Sonoma's gown was now creased and ruffled with bloody rough edges which clung to Sonoma's body like dried fish scales attached to her skin.

Carrying only a flashlight in hand muzzled by the predominant cup of her palm, rage burned within Sonoma, wickless, longing to escape. To turn back time. Destroy all directions: north, south, east, and west, Sonoma's life strings, longitudinal and latitudinal, designed and manned by the sailors of the wind,

stalactites of the soul.   Directions which had delivered
only wrecked journeys in Sonoma's life, tragedies still
shipwrecked and with no lighthouses in sight.

Sweating and shivering at the same time, Sonoma
paused while crossing the fence to feel the rocks with her
feet.   Sonoma knew the cobblestone fence by memory,
every rock of it, every crack.   Some stones were sharp,
some rounded.   Some were jagged like swords.   Some
places had mortar missing, ripening to fall, its mouth
about to lose teeth.   Sonoma had climbed the fence a
thousand times over, for years, crossing back and forth.
Each time the fence's cold rocks getting warmer and
warmer, like a slow faucet turning on.   Each time
culminating into a wise secret that Sonoma had learned
very young, that the fence's rocks were a braille for the
living, to touch, to communicate its thoughts.

Crossing the fence and onto the other side, Sonoma
ran for her life into the lush, green pasture.   Sonoma
released her stronghold on the flashlight as it bellowed
out with light.

Through corn rows, their pervasive stalks paving
Sonoma's way, Sonoma ran with fierce luminosity
through the stalks' innumerable paths, tunneled and low,
as fast as her gaunt legs could carry her.   Their branches
loomed above Sonoma like beacons, enigmatic, showing
her the way.   The pasture was gigantic, its wings spanning
five miles.

Then past them, and still faster and faster, Sonoma ran
with a vengeance.

Until Sonoma finally dropped to the ground, a
conscious, unconscious mechanical rhythm beating within
her.

The fall was instinctual.

In the center of the field.

To the earth, where as a child Sonoma began her mystic travels all those years before, travelling each night to foreign lands or wherever the pasture took her.

Sonoma lay there fallen facing the moon, her legs half extended.   Sonoma's torn, blood-stained white gown glistened crimson in the moonlight, sparkling like chipped rubies from the heavens, the universe's way of polishing its precious gems.

Blades of tall, autumn-feigned grass bent like straw rubber bands underneath Sonoma's skeletal frame, giving Sonoma seating. Composure in the chaos, but Sonoma's meager ninety pounds barely making a mold. The foliage canopied over Sonoma like a hawk-eyed parent protecting its young. Calico, feathery fur swayed gently on its frayed ends, protecting Sonoma but at the same time threatening any dark force to dare come its way.

The pasture loved Sonoma, its beloved child.   The pasture had watched Sonoma grow up through the years as Sonoma travelled its contours each night in mystical adventure and play. The dark pasture had at first been a frightful forest to Sonoma.   Its thicket and coppice, however, quickly evolved into a wonderland of magic where anything was possible if only you believe.

Unlike other nights, however, the pasture's mood and tenor lay somber and restless, still shocked at the events that it had witnessed that day. Its usual carefree spirit was tangled with thoughts.   Heavy thoughts of Sonoma, yearning to help her. The pasture was aghast at what had happened in its wonderland that day and the sediment buried beneath it.

The pasture, acutely alert, watched Sonoma motherly on the ground, shouting to the sky.

Sonoma's arms were elongated. Screaming and crying why.

Repeatedly.   A chant of the soul, expressing magnanimous pain. The soul's reflex to stabilize tragic vibrations, tragedy defined as we know it.

Stilled with solace, the pasture exhaled its breath which it had held all day. Its echoless walls absorbed Sonoma's cries, her lamentations indescribable.

Sonoma had found it, the burial site. The gravesite of her baby. Newly born and buried that same day. Buried in secret, just as it had been born.

Sonoma touched the freshly milled dirt before her, taut and packed down. Its cool grit clung to Sonoma's hands. Sonoma felt the hollowness within her. Her emaciated belly. The place in Sonoma's body where Sonoma had carried the baby to full term despite her frail condition, a miracle in itself. The baby that Sonoma had lived for and loved. The child of a monster, an angel transformed. Sonoma's baby had been stolen in the dawn of the morning by Ebetrio, the school master, right after birth.   Just as he stole Sonoma, so many times, maintaining Sonoma's heartbeat only for his own putrid pleasure and employ, nothing more and nothing less.

Still fallen to the ground, fresh memories of the morning played in Sonoma's mind like a horror movie with a pulse. With accentuated acuity, Sonoma could hear and see all of the moments and the terror that connected them.

"Too many mouths to feed," Ebetrio yelled while trying to justify his inhumanity as he cut the umbilical cord with an ax.

Sonoma shrieked in agony. Blood cascaded the walls.

Sonoma's arms were tied down. Sonoma kicked and fought Ebetrio with violence, surpassing her physical might.   Striving to rescue her child, her newborn daughter, with every ounce of her being, every avenue reachable and those not in reach.

With one hand, Sonoma's baby in the other, Ebetrio struck Sonoma brutally in the head with the thick arm of the metal axe.

Blood surged from the blow, covering Sonoma's face, sheets, and the floor. In the film of the warm blood, Sonoma captured a glimpse of her newborn child dangling from Ebetrio's arm.

Sonoma still engaged in the battle. Blood was no longer iconic of pain but a path to survival. Sonoma's newborn baby screamed helplessly in the background.

Ebetrio's staff rushed in to incapacitate Sonoma, forcefully injecting Sonoma with drugs and more drugs, to conceal the concealed. Sonoma heard sounds of needles penetrating her, feeling the stings of the medications as they shot painfully into her veins.

Ebetrio then ran out with Sonoma's child. Sonoma could still hear her baby's cries, but with each second the cries sounded farther and farther away.

Sonoma then began drifting, clinging to the brief glimpse of her child that was now a memory engraved. Sonoma vowed revenge against Ebetrio and his accomplices, and Café Piraza too, Café Piraza being the place of torture to Sonoma where only nightmares repeated. The wind masters would hear from Sonoma. She would kill Ebetrio and them all, punish them severely by mirroring the pain onto them thousands fold. Sonoma would give her life to accomplish it. There was no other reason to live.

Then like the wind, the dehabilitating drugs carried Sonoma away to another land. A place that is hidden from consciousness and lingers in repose and which the living dare not waken. A place that matched the darkness of the day when Sonoma awakened that early three o'clock morn.

Suddenly, devoid of reason, Sonoma's chants stopped.

Like the inside fell out of Sonoma, the painful contents spilled out of Sonoma though she knew not where.

Sonoma felt free…true freedom, like when one awakens from a nightmare to mercifully discover that the dream was not real and that the stalking images had been a hoax, an illusion.

Without restraint, a woman's deep voice then sounded slowly. "Dig your baby up," the voice commanded.

The voice was elderly, mature. No youth was in her sound. The woman's voice was certain and finite, easily audible, unexplainable to what man calls reason, man's barrier to other realms.

Sonoma fell back in shock. The superfluous, bushy grass cradled Sonoma's whole body like a baby bird in its nest. Its brush encompassed Sonoma head to toe, nurturing her with its soft, cotton-tipped branches.

Unimaginable words. Unthinkable words. To Sonoma, a poem from the angels that she had never seen but had always known were there.

The rhythmic words filled Sonoma's body, mind, and spirit with healing light, and the soil too. Like an inverted rainbow reached down from the sky into the earth and unleashed its arching message. A spell of secrets, pure precepts of power, just as Sonoma had envisioned for years as a child in her pasture adventures fighting warriors and warlocks and four-eyed monsters, where anything was possible, even magic and happiness too, if only you believe.

Sonoma sat up in the bamboo-like nest that held her, on her knees, feeling cautious fervor in her fingers.

Sonoma began to dig.

Plummeting the soil while trembling.

With intention.

Deeper and deeper.

Sonoma's arms and hands moved in untrackable movements, like they were speaking in tongues, a language which the earth understood as the soil inaudibly cried out to excavate its garden.

Sonoma's hands dug like it wasn't her guiding them.

Digging for any sign of life, any chance for a miracle.

Then a shallow grave, Sonoma's dig unearthed.

A short pause.

Sonoma agonized.

Still looking, grasping. Frantically digging, looking for God's sculpture in the earth, her connected fingers and hands guiding the way.

Then Sonoma felt her. Sonoma cried out in tears. Soft hair on its forehead, little fingers. Soft skin, and then a curvature, her baby's head.

With a gasp, Sonoma pulled her baby out of the earth. A tunnel for the living.

Five pounds, a face of an angel. Perfect hands and feet.

More miracles taking over.

A heartbeat. A pulse. "Could it be?"

Her baby's skin was warm. The grits of the soil that had encased her looked like glitter sprinkled upon her soft skin. Like the specs of the dirt had baptized her with rebirth and were showcasing God's creation.

Sonoma's baby was alive. A miracle of miracles.

Unspeakable joy overcame Sonoma. Immeasurable, beyond quantification.

The baby started to cry, exerting a voice of its own, music to Sonoma's ears.

Sonoma held her child in her arms, comforting her,

rocking back and forth. Dried blood covered both of them, manmade birthmarks moving in unison. Sonoma could feel the moonlight radiating down on her face and upon her baby's skin, magnifying the splendid awareness of the miracle that she had just witnessed. With forced alignment, Sonoma immediately realized that her nightly escapades in the pasture all those years as a child had been real, a dream in reverse. That Sonoma's imaginative visions, while awake, had been breathing, having life of their own.

Sonoma touched her baby's nose, a button nose just like Sonoma's. The child's features were identical to Sonoma. Sonoma was a mother like mother earth, bliss defined.

"Aubella," Sonoma said to her baby, naming her.

The stars twinkled in agreement with Sonoma's pronouncement. So did the eyes of the Indians in the pasture who had always warred for Sonoma's welfare. Its tribal leaders who had already unmasked their headdresses and were beginning the ritual war dance for the safety of Sonoma and Aubella, a collective song that would gradually become more audible each day like a sea shell foretelling its ocean in the laces of its mold. To its listener, both the giver and the recipient, hearing the shell's magic imbued, but the war only beginning.

And with the pasture embraced more vividly and deeper than ever before, like a new color palette enriched its field from another dimension, Sonoma carried her baby farther than ever before.

Out of the field.

To a church for asylum.

Far away from Café Piraza and the demons who ran it.

Never to return to the pasture until it called her back. Which Sonoma knew it would someday do, when the time was right.   When the pasture's seasoning and temperate beckoned her like it did that late September night.

CHAPTER 2

Three weeks elapsed.

The three weeks had been quiet. No word of Sonoma's absence from Café Piraza had trickled back to Mt. Ezeria, the catholic church where Sonoma and Aubella had been staying, only five miles away.

Eerie, Sonoma thought. That the orphanage that had enslaved her for sixteen years hadn't erupted like Sonoma had envisioned, that Ebetrio hadn't come rampaging looking for his prized possession, Sonoma herself. The quiet before a storm, Sonoma thought as fear-stricken thoughts fanned her mind. Sonoma fixated in worry about Aubella and what Ebetrio would do if he knew that she were alive. Sonoma thought nothing of her own fate, only that of Aubella's safety and wellbeing.

Sonoma sat in the rocking chair at Mt. Ezeria, rocking Aubella back and forth as she slept soundly in her arms.

The window above Sonoma was slightly open. A gentle autumn breeze glided in smelling of hints of fresh cinnamon. Fall leaves rustled outside in playful discord, tossing about in the grass like children playing football on a calm Sunday afternoon.

Sonoma stroked Aubella's back, feeling the soft cotton of her ivory gown. Sonoma thought about the three weeks that had passed since their arrival at Mt. Ezeria, the two century old church in which its director, Mother Agnes, had lovingly housed them for protection. Mother Agnes was the eldest of the many nuns at the church.

Mother Agnes came into the room where Sonoma was rocking wearing her usual gentle brand of kindness that Mother Agnes always showed to Sonoma.

"It's been three weeks," Mother Agnes said while sitting down in a rocking chair next to Sonoma. "It's now close to the end of October."

Mother Agnes started to rock slowly with Sonoma.

Aubella made a short, whimsical whimper, briefly stirred by Mother Agnes' presence.

Sonoma continued rocking in silence knowing the question was coming.

"Have you decided what you are going to do?" Mother Agnes asked Sonoma gently, her hands crossed in her lap.

"No, I haven't. I don't know what to do."

Sonoma exhaled a loud sigh. "No one has come looking for me. Not even Ebetrio, which surprises me greatly."

"I am sure that they're looking for you. I've known Ebetrio a long time. He's not one to stop in his pursuits for any reason as long as I've known him."

Sonoma looked down, her skeletal cheeks showing more color than years past given the three weeks of healthy nutrition that she had received at Mt. Ezeria.

"I know that it's hard," Mother Agnes said to Sonoma. "But Ebetrio will come looking for you. And when he finds you, he will take Aubella, like before."

Sonoma rocked quietly for a few minutes, pondering Mother Agnes' words.

The two shared in the silence. Like the silence was a way out from the noise that both of them were hearing and feeling but couldn't stop.

Mother Agnes then interrupted the silence. "Miracles happen. You know that first hand, child. But you must be cognizant of reality. Ebetrio will find you and take you, and he will kill Aubella. Ebetrio has killed other babies. I know. After Ebetrio does it, he buries the body long enough for his group to come get it. By now, Ebetrio knows that Aubella is gone from the ground and that she must be alive with you."

Mother Agnes sobbed in her hands, tears bouncing off of her fingers as she wrung them nervously in her lap. "Sonoma, you must continue to protect Aubella, and I can help you. But you must follow my plan without question. You will have to part ways with Aubella for a short while…like a parting of the sea. When the landscape is ready, I will place you back together. Do you understand me, child?"

Sonoma felt a crush in her heart at the thought of leaving Aubella. Mother Agnes read Sonoma's mind, feeling the energy of Sonoma's shatter.

"You're not abandoning Aubella," Mother Agnes said firmly, staring straight into Sonoma's eyes. "You're saving her. Her very life. From Ebetrio, from Café Piraza, from all of them. You must trust in my guidance. I will return Aubella to you when the danger clears."

Mother Agnes left the room.

The afternoon air continued to pleasantly hum through the window, unphased by and mismatched to the gravity of the moment. Sonoma sensed new disaster at bay.

Unthinkable, unfathomable, to leave her baby, Sonoma thought. She would not do it. She could not do it under any circumstances. Would necessity mandate Aubella's separation like it had prefaced her birth? Aubella was Sonoma's child, her newborn daughter. Sonoma had fought to save and protect Aubella, the child of miracles whose life began with defied logic.

Thoughts raced through Sonoma's mind, intricate circuitry in process.

To save her… The words repeated in Sonoma's mind over and over, realization taking form.

With the room's door half open, Sonoma suddenly heard loud, clamoring knocks coming from the main entranceway of Mt. Ezeria, only a short hallway away.

Mt. Ezeria's colossal red doors shook from the thunderous pounds of the volatile person outside demanding to be heard.

A swarm of ladies scurried through the foyer with whispers and low voices.

Sonoma stood from the chair. Aubella was still asleep in her arms. Sonoma peered out through the cracked door with a squinted view of the entranceway.

Mother Agnes opened the giant red doors.

"Hello. May I help you?" Mother Agnes said with staunch calmness. Mother Agnes' black nunnery clothing was as freshly pressed as her voice. Mother Agnes purposefully left the red doors open as she greeted the guests.

It was Ebetrio and state government officials, his crew.

Ebetrio's angry voice cracked open. "We're looking for a girl who ran away from the orphanage. Her name is Sonoma. Sixteen… Small girl. Shaved head. Have you seen her or anyone looking like that walking by here?"

Ebetrio's rough style corroborated Mother Agnes'

memory of him. It had been three years since Mother Agnes had last seen him.

"Ebetrio, I didn't recognize you. So wonderful to see you," Mother Agnes said with a newly inspired voice, like a musical key spiraling upward in delight.

Mother Agnes' body language heralded toward Ebetrio. Ebetrio was not interested in conversation not pertaining to the purpose of his visit.

With pause, Mother Agnes then jolted. "What? A young girl, did you say?" she pondered. "No, can't say that I have. Haven't seen any young girl. I'll keep the lookout though." With brief hesitation, Mother Agnes purposefully rambled, "Would you like to come in for water or tea, or I could make some…?"

"No," Ebetrio said harshly, cutting Mother Agnes off in mid-sentence, decapitating her string of words. Ebetrio spit on the ground, his venom almost striking Mother Agnes' shoe. Ebetrio walked away furiously with an anger heightening in each step, then climbed into the passenger side of a dusty military jeep covered with government tags. Ebetrio's crew loaded in after him, following his lead. Ebetrio was the leader of the group, but his associates were equally as wicked.

The driver started the engine. Black smoke billowed out from the back of the dust-covered jeep. The driver then abrasively stripped the gears and revved the engine as Ebetrio and the others sped off in volatility. Mother Agnes straightened her headdress and politely waved to Ebetrio until the dissonant, jarring vehicle was finally gone from her view. The short meeting had drained Mother Agnes' energy, making her feel weak.

Mother Agnes took a deep breath to try to regain her composure. The remnant dust in the air choked her as she walked back into Mt. Ezeria. Mother Agnes coughed uncontrollably and braced a wall to balance herself as she slowly shut the red doors. Her elderly age of eighty-nine was tolling when combined with the sheer evil that she had just encountered. "Ashes to ashes, dust to dust," Mother Agnes said intermittently in the voracious coughs.

Sonoma walked out into the foyer. Aubella was still asleep in her arms. Sonoma had heard the conversation and including Ebetrio's malevolent voice.

The other nuns rushed to Mother Agnes' side and walked her to a nearby chair to sit down.

"I'm fine, my family of angels," Mother Agnes said with an emerging glimmer and smile as she sat. An afternoon sun strip painted the tile floor with a wide brush where Mother Agnes was sitting. The sunshine streamed in through the foyer window warming Mother Agnes' body and feet like a battery being recharged. Another sign, Sonoma knew.

Mother Agnes and the other nuns then conversed quietly to themselves for a few minutes. Low chatter buzzed amongst and between them.

Sonoma sat down on the floor, still holding Aubella. Sonoma couldn't make out the words but could feel trepidation in their sounds.

Mother Agnes then spliced the conversation loudly with the phrase "Time is running out."

A stray remark in the chatter rang out, "Action must be taken."

The nuns' energy was increasing and into a bee nest of activity.

Sonoma held Aubella, still asleep in her arms, listening quietly as the nuns' meeting ended with resolution. Sonoma knew that the decision had been made and that there would be no more debate or delusion. Sonoma would have to leave Aubella with Mother Agnes at Mt.

Ezeria in order to save Aubella's life. Sonoma would have to allow fate to take over, once again. No sixteen year old girl with a child in Argentina would ever go unnoticed, and if Ebetrio found Sonoma, then Aubella would be found too and killed.

The nuns got down on the floor and embraced Sonoma and Aubella. Holding them, crying with them, huddled together on the floor which was being warmed by the fresh golden sun pouring in like sheets and painting them all with wide, eclipsing brushes. Mother Agnes remained seated in the chair like she was sitting on a throne overseeing it all, which she was.

Sonoma would flee Argentina in seven days with the help and direction of Mother Agnes. Strict instructions had been given to Sonoma to ask no questions at all. Mother Agnes would keep Aubella at Mt. Ezeria, hidden from Ebetrio, until the time was right for Sonoma and Aubella to be reunited. Mother Agnes' plan was both a mystery and edict that Sonoma would follow.

CHAPTER 3

Seven days later, Sonoma arrived in Miami, Florida via a private jet. "The Challengers Foundation" was imprinted upon the jet's colossal frame. Sonoma didn't know who the Challengers Foundation was or what its name meant, or why she was being transported to America. Leaving Aubella at Mt. Ezeria had been the most difficult experience of Sonoma's life. Sonoma's only comfort was in knowing that Aubella would be safely hidden and protected from Ebetrio and Café Piraza in Mother Agnes' care.

Mother Agnes had arranged for Sonoma to live and work at the Challengers Foundation, a charitable organization in Miami which focused on training gifted students of gymnastics from all over the world. It was the only study-abroad program that the Argentinean government had approved. Mother Agnes had taken care of everything to get Sonoma admitted into the program. From the necessary passport and government papers, to photo identification, to Sonoma's record of award-winning gymnastics, Mother Agnes had handled the fabrication of it all to the Argentinean government in order to safely move Sonoma out of the country to hide her from Ebetrio.

Upon arriving, Sonoma went straight off the plane to the Challengers Foundation, a thirty floor glass building located on the ocean front of Miami. Sonoma didn't question the itinerary. Sonoma trusted that Mother Agnes' travel plan was the lantern to show her the way.

Sonoma had no luggage. Sonoma's only clothes were the ones that she was wearing, a pink dress and pair of beige shoes that Mother Agnes had given her the night before. Sonoma's only other possession was a small picture of Aubella that the nuns had arranged to be taken as a gift to Sonoma, the picture which was priceless to Sonoma. Sonoma carried the picture of Aubella in her purse, a small paper bag.

Sonoma thought of Aubella every minute, every second. Per Mother Agnes' order, however, Sonoma had to sever all communications with Mother Agnes in order to keep Aubella safe. Sonoma would follow the order religiously.

"State your name please," Dr. Stark said to Sonoma with flamboyant energy. Dr. Stark squinted at Sonoma from above his thick, wiry glasses which had fallen to his nose. Dr. Stark's tall height towered above Sonoma who was quietly sitting in a chair at a small table. Thirty other students filled the classroom. They appeared as energetic as he was.

"Sonoma Lively."

"What?" Dr. Stark screamed loudly at Sonoma, jestfully appearing to be deaf. "Speak up child! I'm old!"

Sonoma looked nervously around the room. All of the students were laughing except one male student in the back of the room dressed in a black suit.

"Sonoma Lively," Sonoma said louder and with forced intent. Sonoma's name was clearly audible. Grace emanated Sonoma's words as they fell from her lips.

Sonoma crossed her arms, feeling uncomfortable and embarrassed. The last seven days had been life changing for Sonoma and in so many ways. Sonoma had never been in a classroom until now, despite her sixteen years at Café Piraza.

"You have to reclaim your voice, child," Dr. Stark said loudly to Sonoma. Dr. Stark's elderly face was as rough and ravenous as his voice. "If you learn one thing in this class, learn that. Nothing else matters."

Dr. Stark then slammed a book down on Sonoma's table.

The class laughed again. Not at Sonoma, but at Dr. Stark's outlandish, gregarious ways which he always exhibited to get students' attention, and in this case that of Sonoma. Dr. Stark was the most favored teacher of the Challengers school which was located in the Challengers Foundation building. Wonderfully eccentric and engaging, Dr. Stark often wore a cowboy hat through the school halls proclaiming that we can all lasso life if we just put our hat on, the hat's rim which will give us new perspective if only we'll look. Dr. Stark looked to be a hundred years old but with a ten year old's level of energy. Dr. Stark had wrinkles and sun spots all over his face and scalp, which juxtaposed with his youthful, hope-springs-eternal attire. Dr. Stark's freshly tanned face contrasted vividly with his bright orange clothing. A clear lover of the sun and energy in all of its forms, Dr. Stark exhibited boundless charisma in both his style and demeanor. In addition to being a teacher, Dr. Stark was the foundation's gymnastic coach. All of the Challengers school's staff and students loved and adored Dr. Stark, but like Sonoma they had once feared him.

The focus on Sonoma deflected when Dr. Stark began calling the regular attendance roll. Sonoma matched and memorized the responding face to each name that Dr. Stark called. It was an obsession borne from Sonoma's years at Café Piraza, out of habit, in case she would never see them again. All of the students in the class were called except for the young man in the back, the one who didn't laugh, the one wearing the black suit.

Dr. Stark then climbed up on top of his desk and shouted through a miniature megaphone. "Groupings! It's time for groupings! My favorite subject. I know that it's yours too. Get into pairs." The megaphone eked out squeaks of electricity as Dr. Stark then eased down off of his desk.

Sonoma looked around the room, nervous at Dr. Stark's command. Sonoma didn't know anyone in the room, and no one knew her. Groupings? What was he talking about, Sonoma thought. Everything appeared confusing and loud to Sonoma, like she was being blinded by a storm.

Students started to scamper into paired groups.

Sonoma remained seated in the center of the room at her desk waiting for the matriculation to end. Sonoma noticed that other students were dressed in navy uniforms with "The Challengers " sewn on their front pocket. Ivy Leaguers of the poor, Sonoma thought. Sonoma knew that all of the children in the classroom had been deserted and were poor just like her, and that every student had their own story, their own orphan tale. It was a fact that Sonoma knew with certainty although it hadn't been stated.

Suddenly, Sonoma saw the young male dressed in a black suit in the back of the room coming toward her. The young man's features were striking. His dark black hair was salient against his perfect nose and mouth and white button down shirt that was pressed tightly under his black suit. The young man's face was freshly tanned from the sun, similar to Dr. Stark. The young man stood out from the other students in the room, although Sonoma couldn't determine why. Sonoma turned around, away from him, in anxious energy. Sonoma then saw him in her peripheral vision about to approach.

"I'm new too," the young man said to Sonoma.

The young man extended his hand out to Sonoma to greet her, to formally make her acquaintance. Sonoma was confused at his gesture.

"My name is Max. Max McCallister," he said with tacitly sophisticated intonations, his hand still extended. "I've been here a month."

Sonoma eyed his hand and arm that was stretched out in front of her. Sonoma deliberated whether to shake it. No one had ever approached Sonoma for a hand shake or any other form of courtesy.

"Go on shake it," Max said, laughing in jest. "It won't hurt you," he said. "I carry it around with me every day."

Sonoma laughed. Sonoma then shook Max's hand, feeling the warmth of his palm and strong, pleasant touch. It was the first time that Sonoma had ever been extended a courtesy, which Max knew.

"And your name is…," Max said, as he shook Sonoma's hand.

"Sonoma. My name is Sonoma." Sonoma laughed again with the same energy as before, graceful and charming, silent yet screaming out who she was and who she wanted to be.

Max fell in love with Sonoma instantly, just like he knew that he would. Max was an excellent judge of character and what he called "all-the-in-between."

Max pulled up a chair to Sonoma's table. The two were now grouped as a pair.

Sonoma looked around the room. The room was frenzied. In each two-person group, dialogue was transpiring back and forth, a conversation ensuing between the pairs that seemed to imply that no one else was around.

Dr. Stark surveyed the landscape of the room, studying the paired webbings of chaos. Dr. Stark then walked up to Max and Sonoma and squinted down from his glasses like he had done to Sonoma earlier, but with a giant welcoming smile.

"My, my, my…," Dr. Stark said, his smile beaming. "It's always interesting how people pair. I'm not surprised, however, that you two paired up."

The room suddenly got quiet.

It was like an inaudible school bell had just rung signifying that it was time to begin. Dr. Stark turned around and walked back to his desk which was covered in papers.

Max raised his hand.

"Yes, Mr. McCallister," Dr. Stark said, acknowledging Max politely.

"We should keep records of the groupings, so that we can map and study them over time."

"Great idea Mr. McCallister," Dr. Stark replied, pointing to Max. "You're in charge of it, from now forward."

Sonoma lowered her head, sinking down in her seat. Sonoma still didn't know what groupings were or what they entailed.

"What's wrong Ms. Lively?" Dr. Stark asked. "Are you afraid of studying groupings?"

Sonoma stumbled, not knowing what to say. Sonoma forced the words out, "No sir. I'm not."

"Oh, I see," Dr. Stark said to Sonoma. "You're not afraid of studying groupings. You just don't know what they are. Would that be accurate?"

Sonoma sunk down in her chair again, shaking her head yes.

"Well, you'll find out soon…unless they find you out first." Dr. Stark then whimsically picked up a book and grabbed a piece of chalk to use on the chalk board.

Sonoma didn't understand Dr. Stark's terminology or what he was saying. She didn't know what groupings were or how they could be mapped and studied. Fundamentally, Sonoma didn't understand why students were being grouped in pairs in the first place.

With blazen, Dr. Stark then jumped into mathematics, writing foreign looking equations on the chalk board. Dr. Stark then lectured about social studies and science, seemingly dropping the subject of groupings altogether the remainder of the day.

For two hours, Dr. Stark's lecture passed like a slow fog. Not lifting, but falling and saturating Sonoma as Sonoma quickly realized she lacked traction in the academic world. Sonoma had always prided herself on being able to read, which she had learned in Café Piraza's library. The library had been given to Café Piraza from the Argentinean federal government. Ebetrio had been skittish about entering and interfering with the library because of its federal government connection. His enterprise connections were not as embedded in the federal government as they were in the local and state circles. This gave the library a sense of security, a place where Sonoma could escape to and learn. Older students in the library helped Sonoma and other children to read and compute basic math, giant feats for anyone living at Café Piraza.

When the class bell rang, Sonoma rose with anxiety and grabbed her purse, the paper bag containing the small picture of Aubella, her only revered possession.

Max rose and followed Sonoma to the door. "What's wrong? Where are you going?" Max asked. "I'm your partner. We've got groupings to do. Remember?"

Sonoma stopped in her tracks. The other students poured out of the classroom in front of her, she struggling to get out of their way.

Dr. Stark sat at his table packing up books and papers until Sonoma and Max were the only ones left in the room.

"Ms. Lively," Dr. Stark said with a smile. "I'm glad to have you here. Sincerely, so glad." Dr. Stark extended his hand out to Sonoma like Max had done earlier. Sonoma didn't hesitate this time. Sonoma shook Dr. Stark's hand accepting and reciprocating the courtesy.

"You're going to do well here, Ms. Lively. I know it," Dr. Stark said to Sonoma with confidence. "The foundation has a room ready for you in the Challengers dormitory. I'm sure that Max will be showing you."

Sonoma smiled with humility. Sonoma was thankful to hear the changed momentum in Dr. Stark's voice. Dr. Stark's kindness comforted Sonoma, and Sonoma was overcome with gratefulness to hear that the Challengers Foundation had prepared her a room.

"Thank you, Sir," Sonoma said.

Dr. Stark left the room.

Sonoma then felt anxiety building within her.

Sonoma's heart was fluttering and pounding, nervous energy taking over, like a flock of wild birds were inside of her wanting to take off and fly but at the same time.

Max noticed Sonoma's discomfort. "Are you okay, Sonoma?"

Sonoma felt faint. Sonoma sat down in a chair. "I'm sorry, Max. I'm new to everything. I just arrived from Argentina this morning."

"I know." Max said, smiling. "I know all about you. I knew you were coming."

Sonoma paused in surprise, feeling anxiety increasing. "You do? You did? Well, then you understand my situation." Sonoma cringed, feeling the urge to mumble and ramble and spit out anxiety-tinged words.

Max put his hand on Sonoma's shoulder, feeling the soft sheerness of her pink dress. "Let's get you set up in your room, Sonoma," Max said gently. "You'll feel better once you're settled."

Max reached for Sonoma's paper bag, to carry it for her.

Sonoma hesitated. The bag held Sonoma's reverence, her only organized religion. Sonoma tried to make herself snap out of it, allowing Max to carry the bag while bagging her mixed feelings. Sonoma stood.

There was no conversation between them as they boarded and rode the elevator to the ground floor. Each looked ahead like they were living in different worlds. No words transpired between them until they walked across the busy, downtown Miami urban street, headed for the Challengers Foundation's dormitory.

"That's the dorm," Max said, pointing to the massive dormitory which spanned three city blocks. "Do you like it?" Max said like an enthusiastic child in awe. "Isn't it ornate?"

"What does ornate mean," Sonoma asked like a statement.

"Ornate means ornamental. It's like how it looks when a flower is embedded into concrete and its bloom never stops, which sometimes happens."

Sonoma gazed down the street seeing the Challengers dormitory stretched out in a straight-line. It's massive structure and stance impressed Sonoma, as it did all lookers who laid their eyes upon it. Numerous majestic white columns were on all sides of the colossal building. Bronze and silver colored rocks were implanted into the building's walls, causing a variant shimmering effect to exude from the building depending on the sun and the weather, the sky being the ultimate author of the building's color of skin.

Sonoma noticed that windows were placed strategically in the building's design while others were spaced sporadically without any apparent design plan at all. Despite the uneven patterns of the windows, the building was aesthetically pleasing. Sonoma couldn't stop gazing at the beautiful creature of a building in front of her as she and Max walked down the street. "It looks like a large ship sailing itself and others in the sea."

Max loved Sonoma's comment. It refreshed his spirit with vitality. With renewed confirmation, Max knew that Sonoma was the one that he had been waiting for…further justifying the many years that had prefaced that moment.

Again, quiet fell between them. Sonoma's mind was dancing in the magic waves of her thoughts. Sonoma had never had a room of her own. The thought of having a room filled with safety…a residence, an address…baffled Sonoma's mind. Sonoma's excitement-filled thoughts were overshadowed, however, with sadness that Aubella was not there.

When they neared the front of The Challengers dormitory entrance, Max eased up in front of Sonoma. Sonoma could feel Max's excitement as Max walked up the marble steps and opened the glass door.

"I'm your door man," Max said sweetly to Sonoma as he opened the door wide for Sonoma, politely motioning her to enter.

As Sonoma entered, the exquisiteness of the lobby astounded Sonoma, taking her breath away. Modern beige leather couches and chairs were placed generously throughout the lobby, accompanied by intricate silver plush pillows that joined in the design. A large black painting hung prominently on the wall in the center of the room with the words "The Challengers" painted lushly in gold, silver, and bronze. In the center of the lobby, there was a large fountain sculpted out of numerous types of rock. Sonoma immediately recognized cobblestone in the sculpture teamed with amethyst, selenite, and diamond stones. Silver colored water streamed out of the sculpted stones in different sizes, widths, and directions.

Sonoma stared at the surroundings in awe. She had never seen such artful beauty, the magnificent silver, sculpted water moving before her eyes.

Max took Sonoma to the dormitory elevator. Marble and mahogany wood welcomed them as they entered.

"This place is beautiful," Sonoma whispered as the doors shut gently in front of them.

"Wait until you see your room," Max said, casting a smile toward Sonoma.

The elevator doors opened on the tenth floor. More splendor greeted Sonoma as she exited and entered the tenth floor space. Crème and silver wallpaper with scrolled designs filled the walls going down the hallway with accents of bronze emperors that almost looked alive. Bronze plush pillows filled multiple sitting areas, like trajectories, coming off of the hallway where students were studying. Sonoma then passed a dining room fit for an emperor. Maroon and gold jumped out of the dining room as Sonoma walked by, its overflowing positive energy almost pulling her in. The dormitory looked like a palace, which Sonoma loved the energy of but at the same time made her feel out of place.

"I live here too," Max said as they walked down hallways and around corners like a maze. "But you're on the best floor. I'm on the eighth."

Max led Sonoma to a corner room at end of a hallway. Max entered a lengthy code in the number pad on the door. The door unlatched. The number "10-444" on the door seemed to light up as Max opened the door with ease.

Sonoma walked into the room. Sonoma felt like she was in a dream. The room was a place that Sonoma could never have imagined or thought existed in the world that she knew.

"How could this be?" Sonoma asked while exploring the suite.

Three bedrooms, two bathrooms, the suite was designed with modern clean lines with Baroque and Italian decor. An original Picasso painting hung in the main bedroom over Sonoma's king size bed. Sonoma had seen a picture it in a book at Café Piraza's library.

Max felt Sonoma's thoughts. Empathy filled his spirit with the anguish that Sonoma had experienced as a child and was still experiencing.

"I've never had a bed," Sonoma said.

Sonoma sat down on the floor in the den. "I don't understand," Sonoma said in tears, burying her face in her hands. Sonoma could not accept the reality in front of her. The sight was dramatically opposed to her past, which she was still holding onto.

Max sat down on the floor next to Sonoma. Max handed her the paper bag.

"It's okay," Max said. "I am here for you. This is your new place to live."

A short silence elapsed between them as Sonoma's face remained buried into her hands.

"This is your new place to live," Max said, "You know…while you're training here for gymnastics. You can live here for as long as you want."

"I'm no gymnast," Sonoma said bluntly, dropping her tear filled hands into her lap. Sonoma's hands were red with the pressure of her face pressed against them, the way that she felt inside.

Max paused, charmed by Sonoma's honesty.

"Well, how do you know?" Max said inquisitively with a smile. "You could be a top gymnast in disguise and not even know it."

Max rubbed his own face with his hands, like his statement was meant for him too.

Max changed the subject. "Did you know that I'm twenty years old?" Max threw his hands to his side. "I'm getting old. We can live here together if you want, forever. It can be our old folks' home."

"I'm sixteen," Sonoma said with a laugh. "We're both young."

"Yeah, I know your age. I got the word on you before you got here."

"What do you mean?" Sonoma said with a hint of relaxation.

"I just heard that you were coming. That's all. When a new student comes to the Challengers school, everyone is informed. It's like a compound here, the people... Everyone works and studies together, and practices gymnastics together. It's a village here. Everyone helps everyone."

"Mother Agnes sent me here. From Argentina. She's a nun there that…"

"Never say her name," Max said, firmly changing his tone and interrupting Sonoma. "Never say who brought you here. They could be killed. If an agent's name gets out to the wrong people, then their life could be in jeopardy."

Sonoma tearfully inquired with confusion. "What people?"

Max stood up, clearly uncomfortable with the conversation, exhibiting clear intention with his body language that he wanted to change the subject.

"Let's get you settled into your room. It will make a big difference. You'll become more at ease once you're settled."

Max pointed to a large closet in the side wall where they were sitting. "There are new clothes here for you…in this closet and the other one in your main bedroom."

Max then remembered… "Oh, there's also clothes in the guest bedroom, for a young girl. Someone left them here. All of the clothes are brand new," Max said nervously, part stumbling.

"For me? My own clothes?" Sonoma said with surprise.

Sonoma had never had her own clothes except for the recent gifts from Mother Agnes. Sonoma had always worn what was available from the Café Piraza wash room.

"It's like a dream," Sonoma said. "Everything that the Challengers foundation is doing for me."

A wave of shamefulness ran over Max, making his heart sink. Max felt embarrassed at his past. The fact that he had grown up in a wealthy community in Switzerland where money was plentiful and no object.

Max gathered himself and then again changed the subject. "Get settled and rested up for dinner. I'll come get you at six."

Sonoma nodded with cheer, but Max could feel weakness in Sonoma's energy.

Max shut the door and stopped himself in the hallway, holding his heart. The vibration of Sonoma and her voice ran through him like shaking bells. Max felt the despondent roads that Sonoma had travelled, stabbing his spirit like painful, pointed pins. The same pain which Sonoma carried with her everywhere, and mostly in that tattered, but smoothly pressed, small paper bag.

CHAPTER 4

Like clockwork, Max showed up at Sonoma's suite to take her to dinner at six p.m.

Max was wearing a white button down shirt, khaki pants, and black sports jacket. Max appeared stately and polished, his preferred style of dress. Max's youthful handsome looks and confident demeanor communicated metaphorically what he believed, carpe diem.

With precision, Max knocked on Sonoma's door.

Three knocks and then a pause.

Sonoma answered the door almost immediately, an almost rhythmic pattern interplay sounding between them.

"Come in," Sonoma said to Max joyfully with poise. Max could sense that Sonoma's tension had lessened in the three hours that had passed.

"Look. You won't believe it, " Sonoma said smiling, pointing to the new lavender dress that she was wearing. "Can you believe it?" Sonoma said in restrained elation. "It fits perfectly. I've never worn a lavender dress. Not even one in my life!"

Max's heart sunk again in shame. Max felt guilty about the simple pleasure that Sonoma was experiencing. Max's whole life had been filled with overflowing wealth, and from country to country as Max lived and travelled with his father in abundance.

The lavender dress was the perfect size for Sonoma. The lavender linen covered Sonoma's skeletal body with flattering straight edges and pearl buttons. Max had selected the dress for Sonoma a year ago while working with his father in Jerusalem.

The memory of purchasing it flashed over Max, and he felt the happiness of the reminiscence. Max was at a festival and walked into a large tent where peddlers were selling wares. As soon as Max entered, he saw the lavender dress hanging on a high wooden rack above the other goods for sale. "How much," Max said to the poor, elderly lady who was selling the dress. The lavender dress hung above her like a mockery of her poverty and poor condition, its cloth statuesque and perfect and she wearing ragged clothes. "Thirty dollars American money," the woman said to Max meekly, knowing that she would never get thirty dollars and beginning the bargaining negotiation high. Max smiled at the woman's feistiness, it further impressing upon him that he had made the right choice to buy the dress. "How about a thousand dollars?" Max asked the elderly lady. "Would you take that instead?" The elderly lady almost fainted. Max handed the lady a thousand dollars and removed the plastic-covered dress from the rack and left the tent.

Of all the dresses in the closet, Max knew that Sonoma would pick the lavender linen dress as her favorite, and that Sonoma would wear it to dinner that night. Max had placed it in the back of the bedroom closet to further test his intuition.

"It is pretty," Max said, intentionally holding back his enthusiasm. "Let's go eat before we miss dinner."

"I can't believe my room here and all of the clothes… It's like a dream," Sonoma said as she walked with Max down the hallway.

Max knew, however, that the dream was still a nightmare for Sonoma because of one person missing.

"It is, I know. You should see my room. It is unbelievable too."

"The Challengers Foundation is a church foundation, isn't it?"

"It is. It supports a lot of charities," Max responded. "It's funny how wealth and poverty run together."

The two boarded the elevator destined for the dorm's dining hall located on the first floor.

As the elevator slowly lowered, an awkward silence grew between them. It was a silence different but similar to the one earlier that day when they left the foundation. Max and Sonoma stared straight ahead at the door, wishing that the door would open sooner. Max thought to himself that the moment was really here, the moment that he had waited for so long. Sonoma thought of Aubella and what she would look like in the lavender dress when she grew up, feeling gratitude for Aubella, Mother Agnes, and the Challengers Foundation. Both wanted to break up the thought strings that were attached to their minds and share them with each other, though never to let them go.

Finally reaching the first floor, the shiny elevator door opened with ease.

Max motioned for Sonoma to exit. Max followed behind Sonoma and the graceful lavender dress that she wore.

Reaching the dining hall, Sonoma peered in agilely

with caution. Sonoma was unfamiliar with the territory, and she felt uneasy, like a lost ship sailing a new sea.

"It's okay," Max said to Sonoma. "You've got to eat, right?"

Sonoma laughed, which relaxed her and Max too. "Yes, I suppose so," Sonoma said with acquiescence.

The dining hall was called "The Blaze." It was where the foundation's staff cooked and served students food. Despite the dining hall's name, its ambiance was formal and refined. It's walls were painted different shades of faux gold, giving the look that the room had different realms of dimensions. Crystal goblets filled a ninety foot mahogany long table with carved curlicues encircling the massive table's perimeter.

"This place is amazing," Sonoma said to Max as she entered. Other students looked at Sonoma, acknowledging her entrance.

"Who you got?" someone loudly rambled from the other side of the room where Max and Sonoma were standing. "Looks like trouble," the voice sounded again. A young male voice rang out to Sonoma and Max. Sonoma stood quietly perplexed.

Max smiled. "Sonoma, I want you to meet my best friend, Peter. He's always tormenting me," Max said laughing.

Peter made out Max's words from across the room. "Tormenting you?" Peter belted out with jest as he made his way across the room to where Max and Sonoma were standing.

Max shook hands with Peter. Formal yet relaxed, Max's signature style.

"He's trouble, I tell you," Peter said to Sonoma, extending his hand out to her. Sonoma shook Peter's hand gracefully.

"Oh, he's no trouble at all," Sonoma responded. Sonoma was embarrassed but filled with gratitude that Peter had made an introduction.

"Max has been waiting for you a long time," Peter said as someone beckoned him from across the room.

Max pushed Peter aside in play, to deflect Peter's lightning bolt comment.

"We're going to eat. Let us eat, will you?" Max chided Peter playfully.

Max led Sonoma into the cafeteria. A few people were standing in the food line.

"I thought that you were new too. And why'd he say you were waiting for me?" Sonoma asked Max directly with curiosity.

"Peter is confused. He doesn't know what he's talking about," Max said with a joking tone, blowing off the obvious contradiction to detract from Sonoma's questions and the impact of Peter's statements.

Sonoma examined the food line. "I can't believe the food here. It's like a paradise," Sonoma said, her attention fixated upon the vast outlay of food in front of her.

The line of food was staggering. Sonoma had never seen so much food and so many different types of food, in one place.

"I'm speechless," Sonoma said, seeing the prolific food before her. "I've never seen so much food."

Max half-smiled in response, he knowing Sonoma's excitement of eating would be a mixed blessing, part gratitude and part guilt because of her starved past.

"Well, you've got to eat. And so we'll eat together," Max said, filling his tray with beef, fruit, and vegetables.

Sonoma's try was still empty.

Sonoma was in shock at the food choices before her.

With a gentle overbearing hand, Max helped Sonoma fill her plate with all kinds of healthy food. Max placed fish, fruit, and vegetables on Sonoma's tray, and a salad for starters. Max knew that Sonoma wouldn't be able to choose from the enormous food selection because of poverty survivor's guilt.

Making their way from the food line to the formal dining table, Max saw Peter from the corner of his eye. Peter was already busy across the room busting out laughing with someone else. Peter was easing that person's tension too, another new student who had just arrived at the Challengers Foundation and didn't look anything like a gymnast.

"Peter is a saint," Max said to Sonoma seriously.

Max and Sonoma sat down at the table. Sonoma neatly rearranged the food on her tray in front of her. Sonoma was admiring the items.

"This food could feed me for a month," Sonoma said in a low tone, hesitant to eat.

Max lowered his head in guilt. Max knew that it was true. Max also knew that Sonoma associated food with the fear of starvation.

"Well, they'll be more food tomorrow. And the next day, and the next day after. So eat," Max said with pleasant banter, again feeling guilty at the sight before him.

Sonoma ate carefully and with apprehension, eating small amounts of corn and fish while awkwardly staring at Max, then the walls, and then all around her. Sonoma nibbled with silent marvel, studying the many food forms on her tray, barely making a dint in the large quantity of food.

Max studied Sonoma's eyes as he ate his food naturally and without resistance. Max was an athletic type who had a big appetite, though Max's sharply cut physique didn't evidence his eating habits. Sonoma's eyes continued to travel around the room, and then to Max, and then back in front of her. Max let Sonoma's eyes wander like a cat examining its new territory. The two ate dinner quietly together like old friends, enjoying peaceful silence between them.

After several minutes, Sonoma quietly covered the remainder of her food with white napkins. Sonoma planned to walk down the street and give it to homeless persons after dark, which Max knew too.

By the time that Sonoma and Max had finished eating, the dining room had thinned. The once erupting crowd had eroded as they sat firmly in their chairs, upright, in the room of departed energies. Still quiet.

Dining staff came and took Max's tray.

The dining staff then disappeared too, the evening disbursement complete.

"We're alone," Max said to Sonoma, dinner at an end. "In this giant dining hall… Like I am the king and you are the queen, and this is our sacred place where we dine."

"It is a fairy tale," Sonoma responded.

"It's Friday night. When students go to parties, to rest."

"Parties?" Sonoma said with inquisitiveness. "I've never been to a party."

Sonoma then looked down in sadness, then up again, meeting Max's deep blue eyes.

"Partaking in ties…," Max said. "Such a term of art… In my world, the weak minded want a party. The strong minded want a part."

Max's cryptic words generated within Sonoma.

"Well, I'm here for gymnastics," Sonoma said with

quick rebut and laugh.

"No you're not," Max laughed back. "You even told me that yourself."

"I'm here for…"

Max interrupted, "You're here for salvation. Just like all of us. But like me, you don't know what it is."

Max's peculiar statement resonated with Sonoma in a contextual type of way. Sonoma understood Max's statement despite its form.

"Look, there's something I've got to tell you," Max said to Sonoma, lowering his head as he looked into her eyes. "It's something of great import, and I need you to know. The earlier you know, the better…for your sake and mine."

Sonoma's eyes opened wide with attention.

Dr. Stark then walked into the dining hall. He was carrying an old tennis racquet with a worn wooden frame. Dr. Stark had just played a game of tennis with his usual partner whom Max knew well. Sweat filled the front and back of Dr. Stark's neon blue shirt, evidencing a strenuous of game of tennis which he played every Friday night.

Dr. Stark lackadaisically glanced toward them. "Well hello Sonoma. Hi Max."

Sweat was streaming down Dr. Stark's face.

"Hello Dr. Stark," Max said in a low voice, putting his hands under the table and straightening his posture.

"Hello sir," Sonoma graciously responded.

A few seconds later, Dr. Stark walked back from the food line toward them.

"I missed it again. I always miss dinner on Friday nights because of tennis," Dr. Stark said grumbling. Dr. Stark sat down at the table with Sonoma and Max, wiping his face with a towel.

"Are you enjoying your new room, Sonoma," Dr. Stark said with enchantment.

Dr. Stark knew that Sonoma's room had been decorated for her, at Max's direction.

"Yes sir. It is beautiful. Like a dream." Sonoma realized the awkwardness of her words after the words left her lips."

"There's nothing awkward about the truth," Dr. Stark said, like he could read Sonoma's mind. "Your room is beautiful, just like you. Awkward is only when we hesitate to face the truth. Or worse yet, never face it at all."

Sonoma pondered the oddity of Dr. Stark's words and in conjunction with Max's previous statements.

"The truth shall set you free," Max quickly responded, firmly yet respectfully staring Dr. Stark in the eyes.

"Ah, that is true my boy," Dr. Stark quipped. "But truth comes from within, not from the external world. We must find our own truth by ourselves, and only when dark turns to light can truth be found."

Dr. Stark stared back at Max, Max feeling the tension.

"So Max…," Dr. Stark began. "You're off to Jerusalem tomorrow to work on groupings, aren't you?"

Max's face fell.

Max started fiddling with his hands underneath the table.

"Isn't that right?" Dr. Stark continued. "You're going to Jerusalem in the morning. Didn't you tell Sonoma?"

"No," Max said with anger in his eyes.

"Have you packed?" Dr. Stark continued.

"No, I haven't had time to pack," Max said firmly and harshly.

"Well, you better get packing. You've got to leave early tomorrow morning," Dr. Stark said loudly with overpowering energy.

As commanded, Max stood and said goodbye to Sonoma. "I've got to pack. I'll see you soon." Max touched Sonoma gently on her shoulder.

"I'll help you pack," Dr. Stark said, standing.

Max didn't respond.

"I'll see you tomorrow at breakfast, Sonoma," Dr. Stark said as he followed Max out of the dining hall.

Sonoma sat there alone, staring at the different shades of gold on the Blaze's walls. The dining hall lights were now dimly lit, making the mysterious atmosphere even more palpable and combined with the different shades of gold that made the walls' depth vary.

Sonoma's thoughts jumped and travelled electrically, forward and backward.

Sonoma thought of Aubella when she had been born, birthed from the earth. Sonoma thought of Aubella's hair in the soil and the stars that hovered over her when she pulled Aubella out… And of Max's imminent departure to Jerusalem, knowing without-a-doubt, with absolute certainty, that Max knew nothing about the trip to Jerusalem until only moments ago.

Sonoma's mind raced faster and faster like it did that sacred September night. A shooting star was in transit, without an agenda of its own, divine guidance in process.

CHAPTER 5

Max left in the early morning hours.

Stolen away from Sonoma in the breaking dawn, just like Aubella.

Sonoma had awakened at 5:06 a.m. instinctively, the very moment that Max's plane lifted from the dew covered ground bound for Jerusalem.

Another piece of Sonoma missing, Sonoma thought, as she made her way through the breakfast line that calm nine o'clock Saturday morning. A piece of a puzzle, Sonoma knew in her soul as she reached for fresh orange juice which Sonoma was so grateful to put on her plate.

Sonoma stared at the bright orange liquid in her glass as she patiently slid down the line. Its orange color was bright and vivid, so very tangible to Sonoma. Oranges were one fruit of many that Sonoma had never consumed.

Going through the breakfast line, Sonoma made other healthful choices. Granola and milk for breakfast and some extra to take down to the homeless shelter only a few blocks away. Sonoma knew that her health was still in poor condition, and that healthy nutrition at the Challengers Foundation would increase her body strength and aptitude.

Aloofly, Sonoma sat down at the dining table by herself, placing the glass of orange juice in front of her. Sonoma was still examining its rich texture, seeing the orange's pulp, its healing flesh.

To Sonoma's surprise, other students sat down next to Sonoma. They were anxious to introduce themselves and get to know Sonoma better. Their hospitality comforted Sonoma's feelings of loneliness as four spots next to and across from her quickly filled.

Sonoma enjoyed meeting the other students. She was amazed at their diverse origins. The students were seemingly from all over the world. Each student had a unique style and appearance, both in their individual mannerisms and dialect. One eighteen year old female was from Ethiopia. Another female student was from Russia. A seventeen year old boy sitting across from Sonoma was from China, and next to him sat a male student from Thailand. Sonoma listened more than talked at the conversations that erupted and ensued between them. The conversations flowed freely and with ease. Their different dialects sounded like music to Sonoma's ears, each student's dialect revealing a unique aspect of their spirit.

No one said a word, however, as to how they got to the Challengers Foundation. Like Sonoma, they had been instructed to refrain from discussing the mechanics of their arrival and reasons why. Gymnastics was the overarching gap-filler topic for all of them to bridge awkward moments, conversations between them touching upon the Challengers intra-country gymnastic training, competitions, and academic study.

Amidst the wonderful conversation and new friends that Sonoma was making, the room still felt empty without Max, though Sonoma enjoyed the camaraderie and new relationships being formed. Sonoma pondered how she could've known Max for only such a short time. A few hours, Sonoma thought again. How could it be? Sonoma felt like she had known Max forever. The single digit hour reality did not comport with Sonoma's intuition and heart. Sonoma could not explain her strong feelings. It was like Max had opened a trap door in Sonoma's soul hidden from not only from everyone, but also her too.

"Do you want to go to the art fair this afternoon?" the female student from Ethiopia asked Sonoma.

Sonoma didn't know what an art fair was or what it entailed. Against her better judgment, Sonoma threw reason to the wind, again letting God take over and determine her course.

"Of course," Sonoma replied, picking up her glass of orange juice and tasting its sweet taste.

CHAPTER 6

The short hours with Max carved into Sonoma's mind turned into days, weeks, and months.
And then five years.

Without Aubella, without Max, without knowledge of their whereabouts or statuses.

The elapsed time felt like an eternity to Sonoma. Sonoma carried a timeless hole in her heart caused by Aubella being away. Sonoma would constantly think of Aubella. Where was Aubella, and what was she doing? What did Aubella look like, she now five years old? Sonoma's thoughts of Aubella were ongoing and endless streams of wonder and love that Sonoma poured from her heart into the heavens every day and every night. The brown paper bag which had carried Aubella's picture still sat next to Sonoma's bed on the nightstand with the small picture of Aubella positioned up against the wall. Sonoma would look at both of them, the bag and the picture, both carrying empty dreams. Sonoma feared that Aubella would never know her mother like she never knew hers.

And Max, Sonoma would think of him too. What was he doing in Jerusalem and why had five years passed without him sending a message? Was he alive? Did he perish in Jerusalem, and why was his room still marked occupied in the school records when it had been empty for five years? To Sonoma, Max was a mysterious anchor, their connecting source unknown but Sonoma feeling his pull every day.

Despite Sonoma's conflicting thoughts, Sonoma had adjusted well to her new life at the Challengers Foundation. Sonoma was well versed in her daily routine through the week, which gave Sonoma structure in her life and helped pass time quickly. Each day, Sonoma's schedule was full of gymnastics and academic study, as well as Sonoma's morning job as a waitress for the Challengers diner which served food to the homeless, which Sonoma loved. Sonoma had pitched the idea of a homeless diner to Dr. Stark after being at the Challengers for a year. Dr. Stark immediately backed Sonoma's idea with passion, and the Challengers diner opened three months later. Sonoma loved helping the homeless, feeding them not only with food, but also kindness and friendship. Sonoma knew almost all of the customers by name except for a few and one in particular that she had waited on for three years.

At night though, after the regimented daily routine came to an end, and on weekends when the Challengers dormitory was bare and quiet, Sonoma would walk down to the eighth floor, Max's floor. Like a ritual, Sonoma would tip toe down the hallway's soft carpet until she reached Max's room, the room number "8888" engraved on his door like an unknown Morse code. Sonoma would place her cheek up against the door and feel the imprinted numbers with her skin. Then her ear, wishing for any sound of life to come from behind it, the door being all that Sonoma had left of Max and his unseen boundaries.

Each time, Sonoma carried a slither of hope that it had all been a lie, that Max hadn't gone to Jerusalem but was in his room waiting for Sonoma to open the door, to find him, the door to be shut no more. Each time, Sonoma experiencing nothing but silence, though with an instilled knowing that the cadence would change. When the door was ready to open, when it was ready to fall to the ground in demise and rebirth, when the hinges would burst open like fresh, spring flowers on a distant, but visible hill.

CHAPTER 7

"Can I get you some more coffee?" Sonoma said to the man.

The man's dark eyes studied Sonoma's womanly figure, head to toe. Sonoma noticed the man's stare, uncomfortable with his eyes, just like so many times before.

Sonoma felt sorry for his efforts. Sonoma's eye-catching looks were as polished as her gymnastics. Sonoma, now twenty-one years of age, was breathtakingly stunning. Sonoma's long blonde hair hung past way her shoulders, shiny and sleek. Sonoma's physique was healthy and toned, her life literally a world away from the one that she had lived at Café Piraza.

The man shook his head no respectfully, once again getting Sonoma's hint.

The man got up from the table and graciously tossed a fifty dollar bill down on the plastic mat as he straightened his hat, ready for the day.

"This is free food," Sonoma said to the man with a smile. "No one pays. Don't you know?" The man waved to Sonoma as he walked out the door.

Sonoma's fellow student and waitress, Wanda, came over to Sonoma. "Again? He always leaves you a $50.00 tip, and he's homeless. Where does he get the money?"

"I don't know," Sonoma said with a laugh.

Wanda spurted out a delightful low murmur, shaking her head. "Yeah, I know. I know about the shell game you play with him every day."

The man was a regular customer of Sonoma's. He had been coming to the diner for three years, although Sonoma didn't know his name. Every morning, the man would come into the diner for Sonoma to wait on him, and each day was exactly like the last. The man was always dressed in his best Sunday suit like his breakfast was a business meeting, the most important one of the day. Each morning, the man wore awkwardness on his cuff as evident as the pin-stripes on his suit. Like the man was disconnected from the world in an indefinable way, yearning to connect, to connect with someone genuine and finite that could understand his unexplainable methodology that he couldn't understand himself and that we all possess within us. A disconnect that Sonoma had always felt too, which was an unspoken magnet between them with a real force of its own.

Every day, the man would say little to no words, and he would eat quietly and humbly. Then afterward, the man would leave a $50.00 tip and smile and wave on his way out. Sonoma would then put the fifty dollar bill in her apron for the next morning when she would silently return the money to him when she brought him his morning coffee. It was the same fifty dollar bill, every day, that transferred between them. The man spoke few words, just like Sonoma, they speaking the language that was comfortable between them as they enjoyed their daily game.

Sonoma felt sorry for the man. The man was poor, homeless, and lonely. He slept on the sidewalk by Desha street, about a quarter mile from the diner. Sonoma would periodically see him sleeping when she took walks at night by herself. Every time, the man was still dressed in his suit, still freshly pressed and smelling like sweet cotton, which was unusual for a homeless man who lived in the raw street.

With the morning crowd now dwindled, Sonoma and the other waitresses began cleaning the diner, their morning routine. Sonoma swept the floor obsessively, cleaning every tile of the floor. Sonoma then mopped each tile spotlessly and perfectly as she meandered through the diner like a maze. It was a habitual routine that Sonoma had perfected, and Sonoma enjoyed the quiet time to herself.

"Did you see the paper?" Wanda called out to Sonoma from behind the serving bar. "It says something about Argentina."

Wanda went back to cleaning.

Though no one knew Sonoma's story, including how or why Sonoma came to the Challengers Foundation, everyone knew Sonoma's country of origin, her beloved Argentina. The country where Sonoma had been born and from which she had come, the Argentinean roots that positioned her.

Sonoma walked over to the serving bar. Wanda was now out of sight. Sonoma stared down at the morning newspaper, the front page chaffed with bacon grease and spilled coffee.

The newspaper headline stole Sonoma's eyes.

"Argentinean Mafia Arrested: Gun Battle Ablaze."

Perspiration rose from Sonoma's forehead. A cool

breeze blew by, chilling Sonoma's face, arms, and legs. Sonoma fell down in the chair next to the newspaper.

Sonoma re-read the headline. Sonoma absorbed every word of the caption like the letters were filling her lungs.

Sonoma read the first paragraph of the article, paralyzed in disbelief.

"Yesterday, in the city of Sanadora, government official Ebetrio Islhus was shot dead while running a mafia enterprise of human trafficking, child sex rings, and the manufacture and distribution of cocaine and other illegal drugs. Along with twenty-four other government conspirators and participants…"

Sonoma gasped. Sonoma could not believe what she was reading.

"…Officers were also charged with crimes of murder and inhumanity due to the murder of children at the government orphanage, Café Piraza. As federal officers filtered in for the arrests, gun fire broke out. Four local officers were killed along with nine state officials who were killed in the gun fire exchange."

In a state of shock, Sonoma lost her breath. Sonoma cupped her mouth, gasping for air, then re-read the article again.

Above the article was a picture of federal officials swarming Café Piraza. Officials were leading a line of children out of Café Piraza's main building and onto government buses. Sonoma recognized the vacant look in the children's eyes. It was the same empty-soul-look that Sonoma had experienced while living at Café Piraza, and which she still saw in the mirror and tried to avoid. Of the despondency, poverty, hopelessness, and powerlessness that resided in the children's souls, leaking out through their eyes, resigned that a brighter day would never come.

Then under the article was another picture, taking Sonoma to another level of crumbling. Mt. Ezeria. Burned to the ground. The caption read, "Mt. Ezeria was burned to the ground in gunfire exchange which lasted three hours. The Dosagos mafia organization had inhabited it for five years led by Ebetrio Islhus."

The photograph showed singed rocking chairs in a burnt background with charred debris littering the landscape. Mt. Ezeria looked like a raged tornado had picked it up and taken it to another place, its destruction overwhelming, burning everything in Mt. Ezeria and including its structural bones. The colossal red doors were in the center of the field, still rectangular in shape but badly burned.

Sonoma screamed out in anguish. "Oh my God! What has happened!"

Wanda came running to Sonoma's side as Sonoma continued to scream out in agony.

Wanda had heard the howling of the wild that too resided within her. Devastating, secret pain presenting, like a turtle facing a roaring lion, its shell about to be engraved.

Wanda held Sonoma's head gently and with care, giving Sonoma support.

The tide was rolling in to carry Sonoma away, once again.

Sonoma would leave for Argentina immediately and with pace.

CHAPTER 8

Sonoma sat up in bed. It was the middle of the night. Sonoma turned on the lamp next to her on the nightstand.

Sonoma's room was orderly and tidy, just like it had been since Sonoma arrived to the Challengers Foundation five years prior.

Sonoma couldn't sleep. The day had been both devastating and exhilarating. Sonoma was insatiably glad that Ebetrio had perished, that he had died in the gun fight and that the organization of corrupt, monstrous officers had finally been arrested. The orphanage children had been saved, a dream that Sonoma thought would never materialize because of the flagrant reign of government corruption.

But Aubella... Mt. Ezeria... Mother Agnes? Sonoma obsessed about each of them. Were they alive? Or, did they perish in the fire? Did they perish before the fire? How could Mt. Ezeria have become an arm of Ebetrio?

The panicked thoughts filled Sonoma's mind. Circular, the thoughts looped with the same questions and obsessions that played over and over in Sonoma's mind relentlessly, without rebound.

Sonoma was grateful to Dr. Stark that he had approved her request to immediately travel to Argentina. Wanda had brought Dr. Stark's written letter of approval to Sonoma's room at midnight along with a travel itinerary, money, and other necessary essentials to take with her on the trip. Dr. Stark had offered to go to Argentina with Sonoma, but Sonoma politely refused. Sonoma knew that she had to make the trip on her own.

The Challengers Foundation would be flying Sonoma to Argentina the next day. The Challengers had already made all of the arrangements, and including for Sonoma's food and lodging. Sonoma thought of her love for the foundation that had embraced her for five years. The Challengers Foundation was Sonoma's home away from home, her beloved Argentina.

Sonoma reached for Dr. Stark's approval letter to read it again.

The letter was dated two days prior.

Sonoma dismissed the factual impossibility as error. It was a typographical error, Sonoma concluded. Sonoma placed the letter of approval back on the nightstand.

Lying in bed, Sonoma then envisioned Argentina coming closer and closer to her, nestled in layers of a multi-dimensional map. As the map got nearer, the map expanded and intensified in detail, including the richness of the map's colors and geographical shapes. The map wanted to land on Sonoma, to meet up with her once again, like a shadow that Sonoma had lost but contradictorily always carried. As the map got closer and closer to Sonoma, only inches away, Sonoma heard sounds of life coming from within the map, precious sounds of Argentina, which saturated her.

Sonoma could hear pasture grasses behind Café Piraza moving, along with the sound of small feet treading its strings. Sonoma could hear sounds of birds chirping, the same ones that had sung in the field every night when Sonoma had made her nightly walks.

The map then landed on Sonoma, and Café Piraza opened up like a voluminously layered white flower on Sonoma's shoulder, in full bloom. Indians with brown tepees were in the ruffles of its many petals, the flower's rooms. Salty smoke was rising from their fires which were celebratory in nature, not to warm their flesh but warm their souls. Sonoma thought of Aubella, hope at the surface of it all.

"I'm starting to dream again. God, please let me sleep."

Sonoma turned off the lamp.

Darkness engulfed her.

Sleep did not.

Again, Sonoma thought of Aubella, wondering if she were alive. And Max... Sonoma pondered Max's absence with agitation. Sonoma was leaving tomorrow for Argentina, and Sonoma didn't know when she would return. Sonoma didn't know if she would ever see Max again, if their walks of life would ever come back together. In the past five years, Max had not returned to the Challengers Foundation or contacted Sonoma in any way. Contacting Sonoma would have been easy. Simple, no doubt. An email. A postcard. A letter or internet message... Anything. Sonoma justified Max's omission by the shroud of secrecy which pervaded the Challengers Foundation, the mysteries that were attached to the building and the persons who filled it.

Sonoma opened her nightstand drawer and pulled out a pencil and white linen paper. Sonoma often drew marks on the paper at night with the lights off, just to hear and feel the lead designs move with her hands. Like she was making a blind sculpture in the night, each twist and turn of her hand on the linen paper a secret path back to Aubella, as calculated and measured as the cracks and crevices of her palm. Building a sculpture that codifies law for the living, that designs are always at play in our lives - with guiding direction - and that messages can be interpreted from them when darkness falls.

Sonoma turned back on the lamp. Sonoma wanted to write.

"Dear Max," Sonoma wrote, beginning a letter to him.

Sonoma paused as the words flowed to her from nowhere.

Sonoma wrote the words "Where did you go? Why did you leave?"

Sonoma then erased the words. The linen paper fought to retain them, its threads bending with determination to keep the words' structure and content.

Sonoma wrote the words again, writing anew but with trace over the remnant letters on the linen paper, the verbal structure longing to be expressed.

"Where did you go? Why did you leave?" Sonoma wrote again. "Where is my Aubella and Mother Agnes?"

Sonoma's flow carried her further. "Why did you come into my life only to fly away?" Like a child, Sonoma drew a heart after the word "away," signifying love. Sonoma then erased the heart, but it's vestige was still visible.

Sonoma continued writing. "I am leaving to find Aubella. I am being called to perform this task though there is no distance in love and love needs no bridge, no carry. I thank you for helping me here. I am going back to Argentina. I will always be waiting for you, no matter where you are or where my sail takes me."

Sonoma then signed her name to the letter in a way that she had never done before. Sonoma's typical handwriting was small and restrained. Sonoma signed her name with lavish loops, an almost oxymoron as to how she thought of herself. The new design made sense to Sonoma at that moment, full of free flowing ribbons, thick instead of thin, bold instead of frail.

Sonoma would place the note under Max's door before she boarded the plane for Argentina, which was scheduled for the break of dawn, only a few hours away.

With the light still on, Sonoma turned and looked at the brown paper bag on the nightstand next to her bed.

Sonoma stared at the bag's rough, yet preserved condition. The bag, though furrowed from use, was pressed like fresh dough with precision and structure.

"My Aubella," Sonoma said to herself, staring at Aubella's picture in the center of the bag, which faced her postured against the wall.

CHAPTER 9

In somber solitude, Sonoma stood in front of the remains of Mt. Ezeria.

Sonoma surveyed the field.

Now desolate.

Now passed.

The fire had destroyed everything at Mt. Ezeria. No structure remained.

Sonoma's eyes moved slowly through the thick, frenzied ruins. Small fiery ignitions were still active, appearing like glowing fireflies. Small patches of smoke waned like horses' tails fanning out into the cool November blue sky.

Sonoma traced items with her eyes in the charred field, connecting items to memories that were encapsulated within her, ruins too fighting to live.

Sonoma saw two oak rocking chairs, partly burned and broken. Spokes were sticking out of them like knives. They were the same chairs in which Mother Agnes and Sonoma had sat, Sonoma gliding through the air while Aubella slept peacefully in her arms. The memory then dissipated back into the unseen crevices of Sonoma's heart, a knife-ridden rocking chair itself.

The red doors. Sonoma saw Mt. Ezeria's red doors. The red doors were positioned on their sides in the ashy field of muscular debris. The doors looked like they were crawling, begging for life. Like they were inhaling and exhaling their last breaths, beckoning for someone to pick them up, give them another chance at life from the cold but hot fertile ground. Save them.

The cool November sky loomed above Sonoma. Blue and gray hues mixed together, a shade of the heavens, devoid of clouds or any threat of storm.

Sonoma sat down on the ground in a brown, grassy patch next to her rental car, Sonoma's only companion.

It was quiet. Sonoma's acuity strengthened in the thick silence around her. Sonoma heard jumps and shifts by the remnant fires burning before her.

A black bird flew over Sonoma. A sign of good luck, Sonoma knew.

A chainsaw rang out ominously in the distance. Its tunes were jagged and viscous, its shouts getting louder and closer together like it wanted to assault but also bind with the assaulted, the unbalanced instrument that it was.

A flock of birds flew over Sonoma's head in uniform, grand design. The sight was a living tapestry in motion, embroidery of the sky.

Then out of the blue, from the place called nowhere where everything is born, a woman appeared beside Sonoma next to the rental car. No sign existed as to how the woman got there. The neighboring fields were vacant and desolate, and the driveway was a quarter mile long.

"Child, are you okay?" the woman asked.

The woman looked sixty years old and wore a long purple coat with hand-sewn red roses on the sleeves.

Sonoma stood and jumped back, startled.

"Who are you?" Sonoma asked. "How did you get here?"

"I was walking by and saw you. I thought that you could use the company."

The woman knew that her story wasn't plausible. The woman pulled her long purple coat together, the late afternoon air brisk. "Didn't you know about the fire? It happened so quickly. The gunfire and all."

Sonoma didn't respond. Sonoma shook the dust from her clothes. "I'm Sonoma Lively," Sonoma said, extending her hand out to the lady in courtesy.

The woman shook Sonoma's hand, but with an underlying negativity that Sonoma could feel. The woman didn't give her name in reciprocity. "Thanks. Nice to meet you," the woman said reluctantly, devoid of authenticity, only full of form.

Quickly changing back to the subject, the woman asked Sonoma, "Who are you looking for here?" Harsh intonation filled the woman's words, matching the entrenched wrinkles in her face which moved when she spoke.

"Aubella, who is my child. And Mother Agnes, a nun who lived here."

"Oh. Didn't you know? Mother Agnes left five years ago, right after the autumn season."

"What? Are you sure?"

Sonoma couldn't process the words that she was hearing.

"Where did they go?" Sonoma asked with ferocity. Intense relief then filled Sonoma's body and soul that Aubella and Mother Agnes hadn't been in the fire.

"I saw them all moving, but I don't know where they went. They left in the night after the autumn season.

There were carloads of them."

"Have you seen them since?"

"No. Mt. Ezeria got taken over by Ebetrio and his crew. Ebetrio used this place as his headquarters. I kept my business to myself. I didn't want their terror. I've got my own."

Sonoma suddenly felt an out of the ordinary, overflowing urge to get in the car and drive away. Just drive…farther and farther, wherever the roads took her until Sonoma found them, Aubella and Mother Agnes.

"Mother Agnes is dead," the woman said with darkness in her voice.

"What!" Sonoma yelled.

"She died last year. I heard it in town. Died of old age, supposedly, but I think something bad happened to her."

"Where was Mother Agnes living when she died? What city? What place?"

"I don't know."

The woman then started shaking with affliction, like the fire of Mt. Ezeria was now burning within her, the flames torching her every window, every part of her spirit.

"What's is wrong with you!" Sonoma yelled at the woman.

Sonoma could feel darkness and rage present. Sonoma's intuition was taking over and telling her to leave.

Sonoma ran and got into the rental car and locked the doors. The woman yelled profanities as Sonoma started the engine.

"Where are you going!" the woman shouted. The woman's voice was loud and screeching, like a depraved owl in distress.

The woman was now shadowy. Her purple coat had

turned black. "Where are you going, you sinner! You fool!" the woman screamed to Sonoma.

Sonoma threw the gear shift in reverse and slammed her foot on the accelerator, plowing down the drive in reverse.

The woman cursed Sonoma with her fists in the air. The woman's voice was still audible despite the car's haul. The woman was screaming, and with a gurgling growl, waving her fists in the air crazily like she was about to throw stones.

Instinctually, Sonoma knew… The woman had caused the wreckage, the fire at Mt. Ezeria.

The woman now out of sight, and Mt. Ezeria too, Sonoma slowed her pace as she pulled out of Mt. Ezeria. Sonoma was headed for Café Piraza. Sonoma didn't know what she would find at Café Piraza, if anything, that would help her find Aubella and Mother Agnes, but Sonoma felt compelled to go there.

The five mile drive to Café Piraza was painful. Sonoma was filled with thankfulness that Aubella and Mother Agnes hadn't been in the fire. Sonoma was overcome with sadness, however, that Aubella and Mother Agnes were hidden away and she didn't know where. Sonoma wondered if Mother Agnes had died like the ill-minded woman had proclaimed.

Sonoma pulled up to the driveway of Café Piraza, the path that led to the prison that God had earmarked for Sonoma at birth to call home.

Sonoma put the car in park, leaving the engine on. She had to mentally prepare herself before taking the dive down - and then ascendingingly up - the long driveway of Café Piraza.

Suddenly, a long dark limousine pulled up next to Sonoma.

Sonoma could hear both vehicles' engines running together, their breaths moving in unison. Sonoma was frightened and anxious. No other cars were in sight.

The long, pristine black car looked polarized to the poverty of the rural surrounding, the backdrop of Café Piraza.

The back passenger door aligned with Sonoma's window.

The black window rolled down.

"Waiting for me?" a sweet male voice spilled out.

Sonoma jumped back at the words, almost dislodging the gear shift. Sonoma was thrilled. It was the voice that Sonoma had longed to hear. The voice that she knew.

It was Max.

"Max! It is you!" Sonoma said with exhilaration and joy.

Max's face was exactly the same. There was no change in it at all. Sonoma had missed Max more than words could say.

"I heard that you met Gilda, my crazy spy up near Mt. Ezeria."

"What? Your what?" Sonoma stammered.

Sonoma was so elated to see Max that she could barely speak. Like a storybook was unfolding in front of her eyes. Sonoma couldn't believe what she was seeing.

"I got your letter…right after you left for Argentina two days ago. Funny how timing is everything," Max said.

Sonoma's body chilled from head to toe.

Max got out of the limousine, as did Sonoma, overjoyed. Max embraced Sonoma with passion, which was reciprocated in kind.

"I have someone coming to get your rental car. Come with me, will you?" Max said to Sonoma with excitement.

"Yes!" Sonoma screamed with joy. Sonoma felt magic in the moment, which there truly was.

Getting into the limousine with Max in front of Café Piraza was like a fairytale without the fairies. It was real, as real as real ever could be, though not in the way that Sonoma had ever imagined. It was better. The universe had better plans for Sonoma than she could ever write herself. The moment was a turning point, Sonoma knew. The crossroad was there, and Sonoma was ready to take the turn.

Immediately, Max and Sonoma dove into thick conversation. About the past five years at the Challengers and in Jerusalem... What they had done and accomplished... How things had changed. The two mingled like wildflowers, without any type of restraint. The two were genuinely happy to be together, their years of living apart finally at an end and which both of them had yearned for.

"Your letter was the first thing that I saw when I opened my door. Thank you for remembering me, not forgetting."

"Forget? With you, forgetting is impossible."

Max had booked early dinner reservations at The Inn, the nicest hotel around.

"I want us to have dinner. Will you join me?"

Max glowed with incalculable happiness.

"Only if there are no more excursions out of the country."

"Agreed," Max said.

The day had been the best day of Max's life, but also the worst, if only Sonoma knew.

CHAPTER 10

When they arrived at The Inn, Sonoma was surprised to learn that Max had already reserved two hotel rooms and dinner for two. The pre-registration perplexed Sonoma since Max had only found her a little over an hour before.

Having some time before dinner, Max wanted to view the hotel rooms. He wanted to see the design of each room, which wasn't unusual. Max was a lover of designs by nature, though his masculine ego would never allow him to admit it.

Each room was unique, a different world of its own, full of distinctive, spellbinding color and both exotic and native prints.

Sonoma's room was decorated in gold. Gold floors, mirrors, and walls adorned the large space amidst fresh yellow roses decorated throughout it. Pictures of Argentinean sunsets hung on the walls next to exotic, African animal prints.

Max's room was decorated in green marble with inlayed orange stones. Pictures of Argentinean rivers hung on the walls next to brightly colored pictures of European architecture and including a painting of the Eiffel Tower painted in different spectrum shades of orange.

Instantly, Sonoma felt that the rooms' style mirrored the artistry of the Miami dormitory because of the students' vastly diverse backgrounds combined with the style of the Challengers Foundation. It was like the same artist's modern-edged hand had been in both Argentina and Miami, two seemingly dichotomized parts of the world, emphasizing world differences but also similarities by bridging common grounds.

"Don't the rooms remind you of the dorm? How can such beauty exist in two different places so far away? Embodying exotic and native is what the dorm is all about, just like the pictures in the rooms."

Max smiled, feeling the magnitude of Sonoma's words.

"Your letter saved me, Sonoma. I should thank you again."

"Saved you?" Sonoma laughed gently. "How can a piece of paper save anyone?"

Max dropped the subject as jaggedly as he had raised it.

The dining room was circular and orange in color. Crème painted wood crisscrossed the ceiling like a latticed butterfly net. An intimate round table was centered beneath the design, along with three velvet crème chairs.

Once seated and stilled, Max pulled out a small box with shiny silver wrapping. The silver box shimmered as much as Max's smile.

Max placed the box in front of Sonoma. "It's time

that I save you. Open it," Max said.

Sonoma paused with hesitation. "For me?"

"For you," Max said as he crossed his arms with deliberation. Max was anxious for Sonoma to open the box to see her reaction.

Sonoma slowly unwrapped the box. The silver wrapping fell off the box gracefully and with precision as Sonoma gently opened its perfectly smoothed edges.

Sonoma fell back in her chair.

It was a picture of Aubella, a carbon-copy of the same picture that Mother Agnes had given Sonoma before she boarded the plane for Miami five years prior.

Sonoma was overcome with fury. "Where did you get this? Tell me right now!"

Sonoma stood up from the table.

"How did you get this? How could you do this to me?"

Sonoma started sifting and rifling through her purse.

Max sat frozen in silence, knowing that the scene that he was witnessing was necessary.

Sonoma carefully opened the paper bag in her purse. Sonoma's picture of Aubella was in it, just as she had placed it there days earlier before leaving from Miami.

"I know about Aubella," Max said to Sonoma. "I know about it all."

Sonoma was filled with rage. "Where did you get this? Do you know where Aubella is? Tell me now!" Sonoma screamed. "How could you do this to me?"

Max stood and gently touched Sonoma's arm.

Sonoma pulled her arm away and walked around the room in a half circle, trying to figure out what was going on.

After a few minutes, Sonoma sat back down at the table.

"Where did you get this picture?" Sonoma asked firmly, but with a lower, calmer voice.

"I brought you your past," Max said sternly and with force.

Max grabbed Sonoma's arm. "I know where Aubella is. You don't have to look anymore. The time separating you is over."

Sonoma suddenly felt sick to her stomach. Nervous anger and rage burned within her. "Where is she, Max? Tell me now!"

Max looked down at the table, having second thoughts about what he was about to do, but knowing that it had to be done. "She is here."

"What are you saying?" Sonoma screamed, standing up from the table. "My child is here?" Sonoma languished in tears. "Where is she?" Sonoma screamed.

A five year old girl came running into the room. She had long blonde hair, just like Sonoma. She was wearing a white dress with pink embroidered flowers. It was Aubella. Aubella came running up to Sonoma carrying a white rose with her dainty, small hands.

"My Aubella!" Sonoma screamed, embracing Aubella with every ounce of life that Sonoma had ever felt and could ever fathom…ever garner…ever experience…ever hope to know. All of Sonoma's dreams about Aubella manifested right before Sonoma's eyes. The wish of all wishes had come true.

"I knew that was you, mommy," Aubella said to Sonoma with a girlish, sweet voice. "I've seen pictures of you."

Tears flowed from Sonoma's face. Sonoma touched Aubella's nose. Its shape was exactly as she remembered. Sonoma felt Aubella's long blonde hair, having the same silky look and texture as Sonoma's long locks. Aubella was beautiful, healthy, and vibrant. Instantly, Sonoma knew that Aubella hadn't been hurt by anyone and never would.

The sight was a gigantic moment in time, and for Aubella too. The moment held carved canyons, and with no bottom or top, and without means to contain the energy within it.

Sonoma stood there for several minutes holding Aubella, feeling the impact of the second miracle that she had just witnessed.

Aubella cried too, part scared and part relieved, that Sonoma, her mother, was alive and with her. Aubella had been educated about Sonoma and most of the circumstances of their separation. Aubella was mature for her age.

Max watched the reunion with delight. The day of reunion had finally come.

"Where did you find her? How did you know? Where is Mother Agnes? Tell me it all." Sonoma asked the questions in utter joy to Max, holding Aubella tightly in her arms.

"Tomorrow, Sonoma. Not today. Today, just be. Be together with Aubella. Celebrate. You've waited so long."

The lunch was a celebration, the guest of honor being Aubella. Max watched in the background, distanced but near, as Sonoma and Aubella danced and played the whole afternoon and evening in joy. Max was mesmerized by the motherly qualities that flowed innately from Sonoma, forming original, priceless works of art, designs by the wind masters themselves.

But Max's clairvoyance stopped there. There were a lot of unanswered questions that Max would have to deal with, and not just from Sonoma.

CHAPTER 11

At one o'clock a.m., Max collapsed in his hotel bed in exhaustion.

The day had been extraordinary.

Max lay there, pondering the day's events.

Words flashed through Max's mind. Powerful, celebratory, mechanical, intrinsic, joyful, endearing, and the words kept coming, Max's mind trying to define the state of being in which he was enveloped. Max's soul was shining effortlessly in all directions that it could illuminate, a state of being which cannot be defined by words but was trying to be.

Max would remember the day the rest of his life.

The reunion had gone better than expected, the reunion that Max had planned for a year involving two of the three most important women in his life.

Max was certain that Sonoma and Aubella had not yet absorbed the reality of their reunion. It was still a dream to them and in a myriad of ways. Synthesis of their new reality would take time. The same matter that pulled them apart was putting them back together, which they would someday understand.

Though it had been the best day of Max's life, it had also been the worst. Conflicting allegiances were at odds. Max had to face his new reality too.

Despite the late hour, Max picked up the phone and dialed.

The phone rang. A female secretary answered with a firm voice, "Stark Services."

"Dr. Stark, please."

The lady recognized Max's voice.

"One moment Mr. McCallister," the lady quickly responded. The lady knew to never place Max McCallister on hold.

Within seconds, Dr. Stark answered. "Max, I've been waiting for your call. How did it go?"

"It didn't. It's not," Max responded in frustration. "And I'm starting to believe that the transition will never happen. The reunion went well, but Sonoma seems oblivious to anything other than the joy of Aubella, which I appreciate of course."

"Max, I assure you that that the transition will happen. It's just a matter of time. We here at the Challengers take pride in our…"

"We here at the Challengers… Are you serious?" Max exclaimed. "I own the place!"

Dr. Stark got quiet. "I understand your frustration, Max. But transitioning takes time. Sonoma will transition, but you've got to be patient. Recall that when you and Sonoma were in class, Sonoma definitely heard the cue."

"I don't know, Dr. Stark. You are the best doctor in the country. That's why I hired you. But I'm beginning to think that the transition will never happen."

"It will, Mr. McCallister. Trust me. It will happen. I

won't let you and your father down."

Max hung up the phone, exhausted and dismayed. Max stared at the ceiling above him.

"Isn't five years enough?" Max said to the vacant wall, the one outside of him and inside of him, turning off the light.

CHAPTER 12

Six months elapsed. Sonoma and Aubella, along with Max, had returned to the Challengers Foundation in Miami and had successfully began their new lives together.

Sonoma could not have been happier, and neither could have Aubella. Aubella was thriving in Sonoma's care and the stable environment of the Challengers Foundation. The two lived together in Sonoma's suite at the dormitory. Aubella had her own bedroom which Sonoma and Max had decorated with pink butterflies, dolphins, and a magical blue ocean mural on a wall.

In the mornings, Sonoma continued her work as a waitress at the diner while Aubella went to the school. In the afternoons, before Aubella's school ended, Sonoma would take courses at the Challengers school, and including courses taught by Dr. Stark. Psychology was Sonoma's favorite subject. The field of psychology quickly became a passion for Sonoma. Sonoma was enamored with the human mind and spirit, studying every aspect of psychology that the Challengers school offered.

On weekends, Sonoma would travel to different libraries in Miami in order to read additional resources on psychology, psychiatry, and healing, further feeding Sonoma's passion of psychology and which was ever-growing. Max would often go with Sonoma, bringing Aubella too, and the three would go for ice cream after Sonoma's studies, the perfect weekend outing.

For the first time in Sonoma's life, Sonoma was happy and gloriously so. Sonoma cherished every moment with Aubella. Aubella was the center of Sonoma's life and universe. Aubella had stolen Max's heart too. Max was always in the mix of things helping and nurturing Aubella. From taking Aubella to school, to babysitting, to shopping and caring for Aubella, Max was always at Sonoma's side for Aubella's care.

One Friday afternoon, Sonoma returned to the Challengers dormitory after waitressing at the diner to find Max sitting in the lobby, which was highly unusual given Max's routine. Max was usually tied up in meetings throughout the day engaged in foundation affairs.

"You're here early," Sonoma said to Max as she approached him sitting on a leather couch in the lobby.

Max was gazing out of a large etched glass window, watching the busy afternoon Miami crowd. People passed by him through the tinted window incessantly like an endless running stream, all oblivious that Max could see them, but not vice-versa, Max invisible to their eyes.

"I am early, aren't I...," Max said slowly, elongating his words. "Today is a special day, and I wanted to share it with you."

Sonoma sat down next to Max. Sonoma took her hand and playfully turned Max's face and chin toward her.

Max pointed to Sonoma's diner uniform dabbled with stains on the front, contrasting sharply to Max's clean, pristine black suit. "We are so different, yet so much alike."

Max's deep blue eyes caught Sonoma's eyes, causing Sonoma to forget his last words. Sonoma studied Max's handsome blue eyes, his nose, and his perfect cheekbones. A masterpiece, Sonoma thought, though she never expressed it.

"What's the occasion?" Sonoma said softly, still staring into Max's blue eyes.

"My father's coming here today. To the Challengers. I don't see him very often."

"Your father?" Sonoma quickly responded, slowly coming out of her fixed gaze. "You never mention him."

"I do too," Max corrected Sonoma gently.

The tempo between them increased.

"His name is William. He's a businessman from California. He travels the world in his line of work. He's a humanitarian and philanthropist."

"That is great," Sonoma responded. Max noticed Sonoma's interest.

"I want you to meet him," Max said firmly. "And Aubella too, if that's okay."

"Sure… Certainly….," Sonoma said nervously but with sparks of interest.

"He'll arrive after dark. I want you to tell him about your studies and mission work here. Do you feel comfortable with that?"

"Absolutely," Sonoma said quietly, her voice and head lowering. "Of course."

Sonoma rubbed her eyes with her hands. "I'm so grateful for the Challengers. It has changed my life in so many ways, and Aubella… I can never thank the Challengers enough."

"Did you know that my father founded the

Challengers, this foundation?"

"I do," Sonoma said. "I saw his picture in the library. I always wanted to ask you about it, but..."

Max interrupted. "You will love him, and he will love you too."

Max missed his father greatly, the man that had raised him from birth to age eighteen. When Max was eighteen, Max took over the Challengers, becoming president of the foundation that his father had created. The foundation was twenty-six years old, the same age as Max. William had started the foundation when Max was born. The Challengers Foundation was William's way of giving back to the universe for giving him Max, whom William deeply loved.

The Challengers was a bright, burning charitable institution in the Miami community, a charity that funded countless humanitarian and religious projects and causes. From poverty to homelessness, to education to worldwide missions, The Challengers was a supreme force in the charitable community not only in Miami, but all over the world, almost an industry in itself. Sonoma did not fully understand the magnanimous proportions of the Challengers Foundation. Max had prided himself by being involved in all of the foundation's events.

All of a sudden, the lobby doors opened and a parade of six men in gray business suits entered the lobby.

A man wearing dark sunglasses and a long black coat then entered after the string of them.

"Max!" the man yelled, taking off his sunglasses.

"Father!" Max ran to embrace his father. "You are so thin. What happened to you?" Max asked his father. Max hugged and kissed his father's cheek.

Sonoma was astounded. Max was the splitting image of his father. Max had the same black hair as William, though William's hair was partly speckled gray. Max had the same deep blue eyes and facial features, and the same gentle swagger, that same docile but forceful style of energy.

"I've missed you, son. More than words can say. By the way, did you notice that I'm early and not late as usual? Can you believe it?" William said, laughing. William's smile was almost identical to Max's smile.

"I want you to meet Sonoma," Max said hastily.

Sonoma stood graciously and walked over to them. Sonoma was embarrassed at her dirty waitressing attire.

"Sonoma Lively, it's nice to meet you," William said to Sonoma while extending out his hand. "I'm William McCallister. You can call me Will, Max's handsome father," William politely jested.

"It is a pleasure to meet you, sir," Sonoma warmly responded. Sonoma shook William's hand, feeling herself tremble. The man looked familiar to Sonoma, though she couldn't place him.

"I've heard so many wonderful things about you, Ms. Lively. And of Aubella too," William said with a tinge of unease.

William pointed to the six man staff standing behind him. "And this is my staff…," William said. "They travel everywhere with me, fortunately but unfortunately," he said with a laugh.

William's staff then entered the lobby with William's suitcase and belongings, heading up to William's room.

"Well, I'm going to get settled in. We can meet up to later tonight. It was a pleasure meeting you Sonoma. I look forward to learning more about you."

Max was delighted that his father had arrived early. It had been six months since Max had last seen him. Their last face-to-face visit had been a three day visit in

Jerusalem regarding a foundation event, although Max talked to his father every day via phone.

When the lobby cleared of the excitement, Sonoma sat back down with Max on the lobby couch.

"I can't believe it," Max said to Sonoma, tears in his eyes. "It's hard to believe that my father is back at the Challengers… It has been quite a while."

Suddenly, Aubella came running through the lobby doors with her driver, coming back from school. "I saw Willie grandfather!" Aubella yelled to Max with excitement in her eyes. "I saw him at school!"

"What?" Sonoma said to Aubella. "Who is Willie grandfather? Who are you talking about?"

Sonoma was stunned at Aubella's words. Aubella had never called anyone grandfather or even close to those words.

"Is she talking about William, your father?" Sonoma asked.

Max shrugged his shoulders, scrambling in thought as to how he could rectify the sudden chain of events.

Aubella jumped up and down in excitement.

"Who are you talking about Aubella?" Sonoma asked Aubella again.

Aubella's pink book bag then dropped from her shoulder. Aubella unzipped it quickly and pulled out a large drawing of a horse. "I want to get a horse for my room, mommy. Can I get a horse?"

Max seized the moment. "Oh Sonoma, you know how children are…the imaginations that they have. I think that Aubella heard me talking about my father, that he was coming to the Challengers. Coincidental timing I'm sure."

Sonoma felt oddity in the moment, like the moment held more than she understood.

Sonoma told the driver to take Aubella to their suite, that she'd be there momentarily.

"We need to talk," Sonoma said to Max sternly.

Max perked at Sonoma's firmness. "Sure Sonoma, whatever you need," Max said, leaning back on the couch.

Sonoma took off her uniform nametag which she wore everyday to work, holding it in her hands. Sonoma could feel the sharpness of its back pin on her finger.

"There is something going on. I feel it. I know it. How could my child recognize your father?"

"Oh Sonoma, that's not true. You're just imagining..."

"No, I'm not."

A short pause passed between them.

"I want answers, Max."

"I've given them to you."

"You say that you searched for Aubella in the Argentinean foster homes, finding her right before I got to Argentina after learning of the fire. But you've never told me the process, or why you started looking for Aubella. Or, how you even knew about Aubella... I want to know the truth. I want to know it all."

"Sonoma...," Max said rising from the couch, straightening his posture. Max grasped Sonoma's hand. "Do you really want me to say? Can't you feel why, yourself? Can't you feel the truth? Without words?"

Sonoma let out a groan, evidence that parasites were still attached to Sonoma and eating parts of her spirit every day. Taking away Sonoma's focus, her energy, the prana within her.

"No. I can't. I need to know the details of what happened to Aubella and Mother Agnes. No matter what they are."

Max got up from the leather couch. Max's heart was beating fast. Sonoma followed him.

Max leaned over to Sonoma, his back arched, staring into Sonoma's face, their eyes only inches away. "I both hate you and love you, if that makes any sense… Because I hate parts of myself, and you are a part of me."

Sonoma shook her head. "What… What are you…"

Max interrupted.

"But mostly, I love you," Max said with seriousness.

Max straightened his posture and walked over to the window, staring out of the etched glass once again.

"And when you love someone, truly love them…," Max continued, "you do what it takes to make them better, and better than yourself."

Max leaned up against the glass window, still looking out, placing the palms of his hands on the glass.

Smudges, the size of well-fed snowballs, formed. Imprints of Max on the glass combined with imprints of the glass upon him, a grouping that Max would someday study too.

"I have connections…more than you know, Sonoma. So does my father. You should leave it at that."

"How can you say that!" Sonoma stood up screaming.

Max turned around facing Sonoma, their blue eyes piercing one another like two blue skies at war.

"I am her mother, Max. Do you know what we went through? Do you really know it all? If you have so many connections, then why don't you prove it by telling me the truth?"

"The story?" Max chided. "You don't think I know? Do you think I'm oblivious to the years of hunger that you suffered at Café Piraza? Or, the souls that were sold there? I know about it all. I know about the rapes and the beatings, and all of the bad. The evil by Ebetrio. The deaths of your siblings."

"What are you talking about?   The deaths of my

siblings? My siblings were not killed. Magda, Angeli, and Matio were at Café Piraza when I left. I've tried to find them. I…"

"When did you try Sonoma? When did you try to find them after you left Café Piraza?"

Sonoma almost collapsed in grief and emotion.

"You don't understand Max. I had no choice to leave Café Piraza. I…"

"You ran. I know. To Mt. Ezeria, to…"

"How did you know?" Sonoma screamed out in agony.

"I love you, Sonoma. That's all that should matter. You don't need to know my past or even how I know yours."

Sonoma sat back down on the leather couch, sobbing uncontrollably.

Sonoma ran her fingers through her hair. "My three siblings. You said they were dead. How do you know…"

"I don't. I know nothing of their fate. It was simply implied since I couldn't locate them."

"Simply implied," Sonoma said with an underlying incredulity. "You can never imply anything simply. That much I've learned from you."

Max didn't respond.

"I'm staying home tonight. I don't want conversation. I'm sorry, Max," Sonoma said as she dried her eyes with her uniform and stood to go up to the tenth floor.

"I understand," Max said.

CHAPTER 13

The four men loaded into a long black limousine. It was William's car, the same one that Max had travelled in while staying in Argentina six months prior, transported via ship, the limo's limo of its own. Its dark windows mimicked the late evening sky which was overtaken by torrential rain and thunderstorms.

"The storm is bad tonight boys," William said as he shut the door behind him. The limousine driver stood outside holding an umbrella perplexed that William had shut the door himself.

Max hadn't before met the two men accompanying his father. Max didn't like the feel of their energy or their wry looks that expressed it.

Max watched them from across the limousine seat as they each scrolled their cell phones with their finger. The word "affair" suddenly sounded audibly in Max's mind, clairaudience that Max was used to.

"To the Pritchard Club," William told the driver with a boisterous laugh.

The other gentlemen remained silent, still scrolling

messages on their phones. They had known the planned destination in advance unlike Max who did not. Max was apprehensive about going there.

"Why the Pritchard Club," Max asked his father, the rain beating down as the driver took off.

"Why not?" William laughed.

The two other gentlemen laughed. Max felt the commingling between them and his father, which too gave Max a bad feeling.

The Pritchard Club was an exclusive nightclub for men, masked in secrecy. Max had heard untamed stories about the club for years. Only the elite could be members of the club, and it wasn't the type of club where just anyone could buy in. The Pritchard Club selected its members, not the reverse. The Pritchard Club was edgy, not the type of place that Max would ever go. It was a place where wealthy financiers mingled and philandered. It was full of gambling, women, and liquor, its usual festivities.

"A lot of laws have been written at the Pritchard Club," one of the gentlemen said as he pulled out a hand-rolled, Cuban cigar. He was a former state senator. Max didn't know which state and didn't care to know.

"That's why the laws are so hard to understand. You're all too drunk when you write them," William said, bursting out in laughter. The three men laughed hard at William's joke. Max sat quiet and reserved.

When they arrived at the Pritchard Club, a man dressed in an entirely black suit and black tie came over to the limousine driver's window to inspect the occupants. The man recognized all of the occupants immediately, except Max. "William McCallister, it is a pleasure to have you here."

The man then motioned to others that they could

enter, the Pritchard's walls appearing like a tall, barricading wall that couldn't be easily penetrated.

The four men emptied out of the long limousine and began walking down a corridor to the entrance.

Max noticed the fence around the Pritchard Club. The fence was stately and ornate. Its woven iron enveloped the Pritchard so that people on the outside couldn't see in, but ones on the inside could see out. The club was in the heart of downtown Miami, visible but invisible at the same time, the ultimate paradox of Max's life. Max admired the fence's intricate design. It looked to be centuries old.

Walking into the Pritchard, a tall blonde woman led them into a parlor with a small circular table and navy leather chairs. William sat down first like he owned the place. Max and the other men followed.

The tall blonde lady looked about fifty, distinguished and cold. "Mr. McCallister," she said to William, "so glad to have you back."

The lady bowed.

William nodded at her pleasantry, acknowledging her gesture.

"I own this place you know," William said to Max and the other men. "I'm a silent owner, like so many other places."

Max was dumbfounded at William's admission.

William pulled out a Cohiba Robusto and lit it. Smoke started to rise in the already musty room, like a fog was lifting but rising at the same time.

Max was still shocked that his father owned the Pritchard. Max stayed silent and reserved.

"I brought you here gentlemen to talk about my new acquisition, a new project of mine."

William puffed on his cigar. The smoke blurred his

face with its shadowy waves.

"I'm going to be retiring soon, but not until this new acquisition is complete. After that, I'm putting my son, Max, in charge."

More shock taking over, Max was shaken, taken back, startled at his father's words.

"But dad…," Max began.

The senator interrupted. "Everything? You're going to put Max in charge of everything? Are you serious, Will?"

"I do and I am," William said with blunt force. "I mean it literally…everything I've got. I'm turning it over to my son, the rightful heir."

The senator was visibly angry and shaken. William's words took him by storm.

"After all that I've done for you?" the senator said, pausing. "Are you serious?"

"I'm dead serious," William said.

William raised his cigar higher in the air to escape his own smoke, the smoke fanning from the table like he had started a fire.

The fourth gentlemen backed up the senator's comments. "I've been your head guy for twenty years, Will," he said with a sneer. "You're going to just drop me and your loyal senator, after all this time?"

William laughed hard at the comment, the smoke carrying his brass overtures like clouds about to release tempest.

Max was uncomfortable in so many ways.

Max put his hands under the table, his usual way of hiding from what lay before him. The nasty dialogue between them continued to unravel like yarn, Max knowing that more knots would come.

"Of course not," William said. "Do you think that I'm

a monster?" William laughed hard again then coughed repeatedly like his cigar smoke had finally gotten to him.

"I've got your rewards in line," William continued. "I can guarantee you that. But if I tell you, then I'd have to kill you." William laughed, his sounds part humorous and part serious. Max knew his father's laughs well. Max realized that there was much about his father that he didn't know.

Another lady walked in. She looked like an actress from the past. The lady was dressed in 1940's attire. She had dark black hair that was curled tightly to her scalp, almost in a corn row, her hair rolled tightly and with formality. Her eyelashes were long. Max wondered if they were real. Max wanted to touch them, to measure them...to see how long they were, much like the elongated pearls that dangled from her neck. The lady walked over to William, eyeing him seductively.

"My William," the lady said to William softly in delight as she reached for his neck. "They told me you were coming. I couldn't believe it. I still can't believe it." The lady kissed William on the lips. William's cigar smoke enveloped both of them.

"Darling, my darling," William said while perusing her body with his eyes and his hands. William then shook off his actions, like they didn't happen, straightening up and then more so, he being clearly weakened in her presence. "I want you to meet my son, Max. He's the spitting image of me."

The lady turned and looked at Max, so handsome and so young. "My my," she said. "He is the splitting image of you." The lady stared at Max, eyeing him with equally generous seduction. "Such a young man in the making. How old are you boy?" she said to Max softly. Max's eyes widened in apprehension.

William laughed, patting her on the rear. "I'll see you later, Doranne. Now, you scatter. We've got business."

The lady smiled and scampered off. Within minutes, Max could hear the same lady's voice cajoling other patrons. Other men's laughs were audible, followed by Doranne's voice, men just like William who were lonely and looking for female attention, which the lady gladly gave but clearly for a price.

William stood and shut the doors. The quietness beseeched them as the outside noise fell to a low hum. William put his cigar down on a silver tray.

"This is serious, Max," William said as he sat back down cigarless, but the smoke still filling the air. William looked straight into Max's eyes, the boy he loved more than life, more than his own life, more than anything else in the world.

Thirty seconds went by.

The two men went back to scrolling their cell phones, present but not present in the very same room. Only Max's eyes were affixed to William, his beloved father.

"I have cancer," William said, staring straight into Max's eyes, their eyes identical both in color and shape.

Max was speechless and visibly shaken.

William's friends dropped their phones, too shocked at his words.

"I have a year. One year to live. Then my time is up. Just like it'll be for all of us one day when our time is upon us."

Max's heart sank in grief.

The other men were shocked but with a tinge of indifference, which both Max and William could see and feel.

"I don't know what to say, dad."

Max lowered his head. Tears welled up in Max's eyes,

longing to pour out. "I'm so sorry, dad." Reason then attacked Max's pain. "I can help you. I can do everything to help you. I know excellent doctors, the best, and…"

William grabbed Max's hand. "There's no need, son. I've been to the best doctors in the world. In Germany and Ireland, and here in the U.S. I've been to the best. I have one year. It is certain."

Max couldn't breathe. Max couldn't swallow. Max was devastated at the news. William's statement was contrary to his father's healthful appearance. William's physique was sculpted and fit, though he had lost considerable weight.

Max momentarily forgot that the other men were in the room. "Dad, I will take care of you," Max said with acuteness. After Max's words were out, Max then remembered but didn't care that they had heard his personal words.

"I'm going to live the rest of my life to the fullest. That's why I'm retiring. I'm going to my cabin in Switzerland, my favorite place, to live out the rest of my days."

Max couldn't speak or focus. The words had not resonated. They were floating in the air all around Max. Max wanted to grab the words and destroy them.

"I don't want pity. I want pleasure," William said to Max directly, with sincerity.

William then smiled a sweet smile, much like the kind that always emanated from Max. "I want to play cards and gamble, be mischievous, be bad. No point living in this world without some crazy memories to take with you when it's over."

As the night unfolded and the doors of the sealed room opened back up, Max felt the devastation grow within him amidst the contrasting lighthearted fun and carefree spirit that filled the Pritchard. Max watched William enjoy visiting with friends and colleagues, and of course women, as the night passed. Max tried to enjoy the night for the sake of his father, but to no avail. Every card that was thrown and drink consumed had an accompanying grief that Max felt increasingly budding within him. Sewn by the seed that William had planted that night, that his father had cancer, death certain after twelve cycles of the moon, and that nothing could stop it.

After two hours of trying to fake his way through motions of enjoyment, Max left the room to get some fresh air. No one noticed Max's departure as the play and banter continued.

Max went outside by himself on the patio to a fleet of tables, each lit by a single yellow candle. Max immediately thought of Sonoma's room at The Inn and the yellow roses that had filled it.

Max sat down by himself.

The storm had passed. The calm had returned. Max thought of his father and the wonderful memories that had been made. Max remembered when he was a child and they'd go skiing in the Alps. They would surf down the mountains together, laughing in joy, as they made their way into the valleys and rivers, never a crash. Max remembered when his mother died and how William nourished and cared for him. His parents had never married, but his mother had been in his life. His mother had died in Switzerland when Max was five, right before their move to Jerusalem. Max remembered his mother and her beautiful face. Max had always secretly wished that his parents had married. She lived in the house with them, though in separate quarters. William had always been kind to Max's mother. William loved her. Max's mother's death caused William severe depression, more pain than any cancer could ever cause him, Max knew.

Max remembered when William had appointed him president of the Challengers Foundation "to help people," William said as he handed Max a giant gift box with the key to the foundation buried within it. Max had opened the box with naïve eyes, his young, eighteen year old spirit which William loved and hoped that Max would never lose.

On the patio, Max looked up into the sky at the millions of stars in their groupings, constellations. Groupings...more groupings, Max thought. Max thought of Sonoma.

Max heard his father's loud laugh. It was purposefully coming closer and closer to him, to reach him. A sign... An advanced type of telepathy, Max knew.

Max had so many unanswered questions about his father. For so many years, Max had wanted to ask William about so many things. About his mother's background... About the Challengers Foundation in Jerusalem... About how the Challengers Foundation got its name... And most of all, about Argentina. Max had never garnered the courage to ask William the questions, questions that needed to be answered but Max had always buried in denial for another day, another time. Questions that had stacked up like turned-over tarot cards waiting to be read.

As Max sat there, alone at the Pritchard, Max finally realized that the questions weren't meant to be answered, the secrets of the tarot cards weren't mean to be told.

Suddenly, Max saw a shooting star bolt through the air, then quickly out of sight. A spiritual firework in the sky for only his view. Max thought of his father disappearing one day too, when he would pass from the cancer.

William then walked out onto the patio with quiet seriousness in his steps.

"I'm sorry about the news, son," William said to Max as he sat down with him.

They were finally alone.

"I'm sorry, dad," Max said with his head lowered. Max then stood and hugged his father. Tears flowed from Max's eyes. It was one of few times that Max had ever expressed tears in front of his father.

"It's okay, son. It's okay," William said to Max, consoling him. William patted Max's back. "None of us die. You know that. We just change form. Remember all the classes that you took about this in Jerusalem?"

Max cried. William cried too. Their tears fell together in the same synchronicity and pace. Max would remember that moment with his father forever, the man who had raised and cared for him and gave him endless, unconditional love his whole life.

The festive ambiance of the Pritchard continued inside, spilling out in slithers. Life was continuing despite the change that had rushed in, its presence now announced.

CHAPTER 14

At eight a.m. the next morning, Max called William's room.

There was no answer.

William had left in the night. Like Max, the darkness was William's preferred time to travel. William had always joked that he moved better in the darkness because he felt like a vampire on the prowl.

Max pondered William's early arrival to the Challengers the day before. It had been a day filled with thunderstorms and darkness, the perfect ambiance that his father loved. Max knew that William had made the trip to reveal the cancer. Max was still in shock at the realization that his father was dying and had only one year to live.

Max got in the shower. The water beat down on his back with intensity, filling the bathroom with a concealing vapor. Max privately mourned to himself.

Max didn't know if he would ever see his father again. Max didn't understand why William had rebuked his offer to care for him.

"He didn't even get to talk with Sonoma or spend time with Aubella," Max said to himself, frozen in the hot water of the shower which continued to beat down on him like a drum.

At breakfast in the dining hall, Max met Sonoma and Aubella at 8:00 a.m., their usual meeting time. Aubella ran through the breakfast hall exuding her typical sweet energy and charming everyone in her sight, and including Max. Max and Sonoma quietly got their food and sat down at the dining table to eat. Sonoma gracefully called for Aubella across the room to come eat, Aubella still mischievously running through the hall dispelling her own special brand of magic to all who came in contact with her.

"It's time to eat, Aubella," Sonoma called out again.

"I'm busy, mommy," Aubella said politely while pulling a jump rope out of her pocket. All of the students in the dining hall laughed at Aubella's response.

Sonoma and Max ate, enjoying quiet time together. Sonoma put fresh fruit and orange juice in front of Max. "I got these for you."

Max smiled.

Sonoma sensed Max's ailing spirit.

"I know about your father," Sonoma said in a low whisper. "I know about the cancer. I am so terribly sorry."

"How did you know?"

"William told me. He visited me and Aubella last night. Before you all left for the Pritchard."

"So you knew that we were going there, huh...," Max said with displeasure.

"Yes. William told me that you all were going there to do charity work."

Max shuttered at the thought of charity work at the

Pritchard. "What else did he tell you?"

"Nothing really. Just that you were his beloved. Those were his exact words. And to watch over and protect you."

"Protect me?" Max laughed. "Yeah right," Max said with a hint of defiance.

"Yes, protect you. William said that the ones who protect others are the ones who need protection."

Aubella ran up to Max, still not ready to eat.

"I want to paint a rainbow today, Max," Aubella said to Max, her sugary energy sputtering out like the paint that she wished for.

Max picked up Aubella joyfully and gave her a big hug. Color returned to Max's cheeks. "Here's my vitality," Max said to Sonoma, referring to Aubella. Aubella hugged Max's neck like a monkey and then snuggled in next to him on the bench as Max kissed Aubella's forehead. Max then cut up Aubella's food for her to eat, a pancake and grapes, accompanied by fresh apple juice to wash it down.

"Aubella loves you," Sonoma said. "She truly does."

Max smiled, knowing it was true. "How can she not love me?" Max joked in response. "I love her too," Max said seriously. "How can anyone not love her."

Aubella ate some pieces of grape and a few bites of pancake. Aubella then took off again, her energy soaring through the room like a pocket rocket of energy.

After eating breakfast, Max looked candidly at Sonoma. "Things are changing, you know. Everything is changing. The life as I knew it, it is changing dramatically."

"But we're not," Sonoma said. "We're not changing. We're together. You, me, and Aubella."

"Yes, you're right. I thank God for that."

And as the two sat there watching Aubella run through the room, the two realized something that they hadn't realized before. They were a family. A family of patchwork assembled by fate's sewing hands, the entire room of students and staff at the foundation being their family too.

CHAPTER 15

The call came at midnight.

Max hung up the phone. Max cried out in shock and grief. It'd been only two weeks since William had left Miami.

William had died. He had passed away only minutes before, dying at his cabin in Switzerland.

Max fell on his bed sobbing.

"What happened to the year!" Max cried out in anguish. "What happened to the time that the doctors promised him!"

Max was overcome with grief.

Max thought of the Pritchard, the last moments that he and his father had spent together. Of William's walk out of Pritchard to talk with him in private, and of the yellow candles that commemorated it.

Max wanted to call Sonoma, to tell her the news. But it was late, and she and Aubella were sleeping. Max decided to wait until morning.

A discreet, subtle knock then suddenly sounded on Max's door.

Max forced himself up. Max grabbed a towel from the bathroom and dried his face. The knocking person waited patiently.

Max answered the door.

"Mr. McCallister, can I come in?"

It was an elderly man in a yellow raincoat. Max had never seen him before.

"Who are you? Why are you here?" Max asked. "How did you get past security?"

"You don't need to know. Any of it... Just that I'm your father's attorney."

"Get out," Max said with hostility, starting to shut the door. "Do you realize your timing?"

"I know," the man said. "I extend to you my condolences. I worked for your father for decades. He was like a brother to me."

Max shook his head in frustration, motioning the man to come in.

The man sat down on a white settee near the door. Max sat across from him in a chair. Max wondered if it could all be a dream.

"You're to tell no one that I was here," the man said to Max firmly. The man then handed Max a large metallic bag. "Your father told me to give this to you as soon as he passed."

Max stared at the bag, hesitant to accept it.

The man was taken back. "Are you kidding me? Your deceased father sent this to you, and you don't want it?"

Max sensed a darkening anger boiling within him.

"Get out," Max said to the man. "Now."

The man quickly got up and left Max's room, leaving the metallic bag behind. The room's heavy metal door slammed, which was upsetting, sounding like a gun blast.

Max was perplexed.

Max stared at the metallic bag.

Max wanted to accept the bag and open it, per his father's wishes. Max didn't doubt that the man had been William's counsel and agent. A part of Max, however, told him that something sinister was inside...a sordid piece of a puzzle to an unexplained matter.

Instinctually, Max opened the door again. The man was outside the door on his cell phone.

"Why are you still here? Get out!" Max yelled to the man.

The man scurried down the floor and out of the building. Like a heartbeat, Max could hear the man's footsteps leaving the building, every step. All the way down the hallway, down the elevator, and into the lobby and outside, Max could hear each step that the man took while leaving, his distance getting farther and farther away until he was finally gone.

Max sat down on his bed, staring at the metallic bag that shimmered from across the room by the glow of the muted television. Tears flowed from his eyes.

Max threw the towel across the room.

Then, Max remembered. It was the bag that William would carry with him on trips that they took when Max was young. Max remembered his father placing important business papers into the bag when they travelled and taking it to important meetings and functions. Max remembered his father packing peanut butter crackers in the bag for Max, and other simplistic essentials, for events and social gatherings when Max was a child. Max never had a nanny or other female caregiver after Max's mother died when he was five. William had been Max's sole caregiver in all ways, now symbolized by that certain metallic bag.

Max walked over and put his hand on the metallic bag,

feelings its designed ridges and glossed texture.

Max looked inside of the bag. In it, were numerous items varying in size wrapped with white tissue paper. An envelope with the engraved letter "m" was taped to the front of the bag. Max touched the engraved letter "m," feeling the silk of the emboss and following the shape of its arches. William had placed the card there for him.

Max opened the envelope and took out the handwritten letter.

My Max,

By now I have passed through the glass horizon. May God have mercy on my soul. Do not bereave my passing. Nothing ever dies. It only changes form. I will see you again when the season comes to fruition, when the horizon is ready to shatter once again so that I can again make my presence known to you.

I am writing this letter to you to as my obituary. It is the only obituary of me to ever be written, and you will be its only reader.

Your mother and you were the joys of my life. I cannot describe the glorious condition that I attained by both of your works and presence upon me. You both filled me with love and compassion, something that I had never before felt until I found you both. I tried to emulate this glory that I felt in my later years of life, though without complete success. Despite my failings, however, I am not a failure. I am a champion, just like you. I am a collector of power and sculptor of weakness. Only then can strength be found.

Before you knew me, I was an evil man. I murdered. I tortured. I took ill pleasure in things that I should have foregone, but did not. You know none of it my boy, for your birth gave me new insight. The day that you were born was the same day that I was reborn. But you must know of my shortcomings now so that they can be stretched out on a canvas and examined, made long, made parallel, made right.

Old habits are hard to shed as well as the consequences that succeed them. However, the truth needs to be exposed. I want my obituary to be clear, and so that you can understand the karma that frames this letter and which I am passing to you now…so that when the torch reignites, it will serve you for better causes.

I love you my son, my precious child. Do not forget me, for I will be standing at the glass horizon to pull you through with the time is right. Be wary of the karma that will now affect you. I can shield it no more.

Your loving father, William

Max buried his face in a pillow, shocked and tormented at the words. The letter jolted Max with electricity, over and over. The letter jolted Max's memory, his body, his words, his mind, his heart, his soul.

Max read the letter again, studying his father's words meticulously.

Murder…

Torture… Max read the letter again, and then again.

Max felt mass confusion at the letter and coupled with receiving it so soon after his father's death. The grief made the ambiance sickening, making Max feel helpless, like one was being drowned in water but while breathing at the same time.

After a period of silence, Max stared back at the letter which now looked like hieroglyphics, a different language. Max put the letter back into the engraved envelope, never to be read again.

With impulse, Max removed the first item from the

bag. It was on the top of the piled items in the bag, square in shape. Max unwrapped the soft tissue paper covering it slowly and with precision. The tissue paper then fell to the floor, as did Max's heart.

"Oh my God!" Max screamed out in tears.

Max felt an indescribable, life-taking wound, like a knife had just stabbed him and his body was in shock, medicinally masking the pain.

"How could it be!" Max screamed.

Grief and hatred saturated his body.

It was a picture frame holding the unimaginable. A picture of his father with a man in uniform standing in front of a large building, a sign "Café Piraza" hanging on the door. That uniformed man was Ebetrio.

Max threw the picture frame up against the wall. Glass shattered into a thousand pieces. The picture half dangled onto the wall and the floor, unscathed.

In anguish, Max fell to the ground screaming and sobbing. Max dared the broken glass to cut him. Max begged the broken glass to cut him.

Max vowed to never open another item in the metallic bag, the secret treasure trove of misery. The breathing obituary that told its unspeakable story in pictures and items, without words.

Max lay there for an hour, slowly pulling himself together.

Max knew that things had to be done, and before the morning came.

Max picked up the picture and the frame, now separated, and wrapped them separately with the remnant tissue paper. The frame would never hold the picture again. The picture would never be bound again. The picture was free, finally free...as was the frame, both wrapped in tissue of its own.

Max put the items back into the bag.

And like his father, Max left in the darkness of the night like a vampire on the prowl, carrying the metallic bag, the darkness to cover the truth that lay within, taking the bag away to another place where it belonged.

CHAPTER 16

Not long after William died, Max appointed Sonoma to be the missions' director of the Challengers Foundation.

No one questioned Max's decision. Everyone knew that Sonoma's leadership would benefit the foundation. Sonoma had a unique way of positively living her life and communicating with others. Sonoma would always listen to people instead of talk - hearing them - and with her usual style of grace and lovingness. Sonoma used softness to push her points across to people. Sonoma had an innate knowledge that crushing force often broke people apart and which defeated the goal of bridging people together. Though Sonoma was the missions' director, Sonoma still helped out at the diner feeding the homeless numerous times a week.

As the years passed, Sonoma and Max continued to live at the Challengers dormitory and participate in charitable causes. The most active causes were helping orphans, children, and homeless persons find homes and receive proper nutrition. Max enjoyed seeing Sonoma making positive differences in people's lives, and including his own life as they spent their time working in the foundation and running charitable events all over the world. Helping others was Sonoma's passion, and Aubella's passion too. Aubella followed in her mother's footsteps. When Aubella turned eighteen, Aubella moved to Africa to direct the Challengers Foundation's missions there, a move that made both Sonoma and Max "proud parents," as Max liked to call themselves.

With the change of Aubella moving to Africa, Max decided that the spirit of flux was upon them and that it was time to fly with the change in the air like a kite, not avoid it. As a surprise, Max moved Sonoma and himself out of the dormitory and into a mansion near the foundation, they residing together but living in separate wings. The move had been refreshing, bringing about a new change in perspective. Max and Sonoma immersed themselves in learning about the human spirit, including spiritual connectedness and studying religions from all over the world.

However, although Max and Sonoma's relationship had grown considerably through the years, Max had placed a palpable reserve between them, prohibiting anything more than business associates and friends. Best friends with a mission is how Max defined their relationship. Sonoma and Max were inseparable but often worlds away. They were always focused on the Challengers Foundation's work and missions to help others, as well as Aubella, but not themselves. Sonoma had written and published three books for the Challengers Foundation, all three being self-help books for charities.

"Can you believe that you're an author now?" Max said to Sonoma while walking down the beach in front of the mansion one July early eve. "Just think of the people that you will reach, and the people that they will reach… Like a ripple in a pond that will keep growing and growing, reaching others."

"If I could only reach myself…," Sonoma said, feeling the sand beneath her feet as the cool water washed over them.

"When you help others, you help yourself," Max joked back, although he was serious.

Like a flash, Sonoma thought of Café Piraza and when she would teach younger children alphabet letters. Sonoma wondered where those children were now, all grown up… Where they were… Where they could be, if they were alive… Sonoma thought of the horrendous path that she had travelled from birth to the Challengers, and the connecting, saving grace of Mother Agnes, whom Sonoma thought of every day. Sonoma then thought of Aubella. The sand on Sonoma's feet reminded her of the dirt on Aubella's skin when she first held Aubella in her arms.

Max stopped Sonoma and looked directly into her eyes. "I believe in miracles because I believe in you. You are a miracle. Aubella is a miracle too."

Max was captivated by Sonoma's blue eyes, the same color of the water and flowing waves beneath their feet.

"Well don't get too into me," Sonoma said, breaking up Max's thought. "I've got a lot of work to do. I've got so many charity book events planned. So many things coming up. I hope that I can…"

"I will handle it all for you," Max said, interrupting Sonoma. "Don't worry."

Max's relationship had evolved into one of strictly business and Sonoma could feel that it was still headed in that same direction. It was more of Max's doing than that of Sonoma. Things changed after William died. Max became more business-like than ever before. Max hid behind work, work being a mask that Max wore everyday to shield him from the pain of losing his father. Over time, romantic precursors between Max and Sonoma became attenuated and then rare.

In what free time they did share, Max enjoyed reading Sonoma's writings and walking along the beach. The two of them often stayed up for hours talking about philosophy, psychology, and the human spirit and in conjunction with Sonoma's charity-based written works. Sonoma realized that they had grown apart at the same time that they had grown together.

"I am grateful for you," Sonoma said to Max as they continued their walk down the beach. "For everything that you do… For everything that you've done… Which cannot even be measured…"

Sonoma turned and looked at the Miami mansion behind her, a picturesque palace in Sonoma's eyes. "This place is so beautiful. It's so much better than I deserve," Sonoma muttered.

Max stopped Sonoma. "No, you deserve more. Much more. More than I could ever give you."

Sonoma was surprised at Max's words, but she was happy to hear them. Happy to hear Max speak to her in a personal way. Sonoma clung to the sound of each word in her mind as she felt the tenderness within him.

"There's something I have to tell you, Sonoma."

"Sure. What?"

"I have to take a business trip for a week, to Argentina of all places." Max rarely said the word Argentina, but the word bellowed of him as if it could not be stopped.

"Argentina?" Sonoma paused. "Why Argentina?"

"It is complicated. I've got some remaining work

involving dad."

"In Argentina? You never told me that your father had property in Argentina or work being done there."

"Like I said, it's complicated. Dad was always complicated. Simplicity wasn't his strong point."

Sonoma ran her fingers through her hair. "I'm glad that you told me. You know that Argentina is hard for me. I guess that I'm complicated too."

"I'll be back in a week. There's no point in me giving you the details. I'll just bore you with them."

Max wrung his hands as he walked, which Sonoma knew meant that Max was nervous.

The two turned and walked back toward the mansion. Max was relieved that he had delivered the news and without incident.

CHAPTER 17

The week passed slowly.

The seventh day came. Max hadn't called Sonoma from Argentina at all during the week.

Sonoma told herself that she wasn't worried. Sonoma knew that Max would return.

"He'll be back soon," Sonoma said to herself while standing on the edge of the Challengers Foundation's yacht in the deep Atlantic ocean.

Sonoma was ready to dive.

A white sea bird flew by, cocking and cooing. Sonoma made eye contact with the bird as it rounded and swooped down next to her and then past her.

Sonoma positioned her hands and pointed her toes, just like she had learned in her years of gymnastics, the fake but real program of designed movements that had saved her life.

Sonoma was ready. Ready to take the leap.

More gymnastics, but in the sky.

CHAPTER 18

The sound of the water brushed against Sonoma as she dove deeply into the ocean, a jet of energy only heard by the blue skies above and the gentle wind around her. The stillness of the water wore rippled designs from Sonoma's dive, and she swam instinctively, without pre-meditation. A pattern of patternless ocean waves that only God can see, hear, and track, Sonoma swam like a sea creature innately moving to its destination.

Deeper and deeper Sonoma swam, descending, her eyes open.

Moments passing, seconds immersing.

The light blue water gradually darkening, darker blue shade after shade, the ocean's color wheel descending with her.

Sonoma's long blonde hair danced back and forth under the deep blue water, like she was searching for something, like a buried treasure or sand covered jewel. Sonoma's long slender legs moved rhythmically with the water, creating inaudible, measurable beats, a song heard by the sea life that swam with and all around her.

Then suddenly, desha vu-like synchronicity came over Sonoma, the universe feathering its memories.

The black-lighting water. Sonoma remembered.

Back flash. Traumatic memory. Her mind's eye. Appearing like a lead-drawn sketch, intricate but in three dimensional form, Sonoma could see herself as a child. Five years old. The child was her, blonde pig tails and definitive eyes, blackened by abuse. Scared and frail, the young child screamed for help, her hands frantically waving, water swirling around her perimeter. A tattered sign titled "Argentina" appeared and then faintly disappeared, as did the child.

Back flash. Blurred movements. A sixty year old man with suspenders. Dirty, his coppery mustache curled baroquely at both ends, a rattlesnake whip attached to his face. An evil, sinister grin. Rooms, many of them, young girls screaming. Vibration echoing out into the hallway where men stood in line. To go inside, their boots lined up, soldiered on the rustic cobblestone floor. Young girls with red lipstick. Fearful gray dirty walls.

Back flash. A baby being born and taken. A young mother screaming in agony. "Why! Why!" the young mother screamed agonizingly from her core in desperation. Fresh blood on her mouth, the blankets, and the floor.

Within seconds, the visions were gone, leaving as fractured as they came.

Unable to reconcile the apparitions with the physical world, Sonoma's direction abruptly reversed, friction bubbling with the water like it was boiling down below. Up, up, from the ocean floor, Sonoma darted. Upsurging like a shooting star, Sonoma swam violently and with struggle to the yacht with her last remaining breath.

Knifing out, with barely a moment to spare, Sonoma grabbed hold of the ladder, fighting to regain her breath, onerously coughing and gasping. And in slow, half-broken intonations, the words "I am Sonoma" broke out of her, sounding like crashes to her ears, pulses she felt on her pale lips.

Minutes went by. Sonoma's breath gradually came to an ease. Sonoma stayed immersed in the water, the ladder embracing Sonoma as much as she it. Trying to understand her expellation of words. Her collaged thoughts. To reconcile the seemingly irreconcilable, in Sonoma's sea of fleeting thoughts, images, and fears. Noise in the quiet all around her.

A large sea turtle approached, undaunted by Sonoma's presence. A colossal giant, Sonoma froze in awe as the massive sea turtle rowed toward her, then close, only five inches away. With a startling shared closeness, Sonoma studied its shell markings, its enamoring code to Sonoma's eyes, its secret language of its own. Myriad, pattern upon pattern, its shell bore ornate designs. Segmented colors, in precise, measured rows, and including silver bronze ovals, emblematic of shields. Indian-style arches, iconic to the turtle, looked like a tapestry of drawn corn mazes, quests to travel from one place to the next without being blocked, a cryptic compass from its maker. The large rounded base of its shell resembled carved wood. Like the turtle was carrying a living tree on its back, its roots invisible, while its limbs propelled it along.

The moment grabbed Sonoma. Cracks and crevices in the turtle's shell, ancillary to the designs, captivated Sonoma's focus. The cracks and crevices were varied, both in size and age, caused from injurious acts, trauma memorialized in its shell. Sonoma reached out with one hand and rubbed the turtle's wet shell as it slowly swam by her. Back and forth, jagged to touch, the cracks and crevices were rough to Sonoma's fingers, bumpy and uneven, sharp in some places like blades sharpened over time, braille for the blinded, God's hieroglyphics. Still undaunted by Sonoma, the turtle never flinched, continuing its tempoed row as Sonoma's hand glided over it, Sonoma invisible to the turtle, the turtle on its own mission.

"The cracks," Sonoma whispered.

Instinctively, Sonoma ran her fingers over the three inch scar on the back of her neck, which Sonoma covered each day with her long blonde hair. Her wet hair to one side, Sonoma rubbed the scar slowly, left to right, then up and down, feeling it. The horrific scar, rubbery and thick, branding caused by childhood abuse, a man-made tumor in Sonoma's eyes, it having a memory and heartbeat of its own. Sonoma hated the scar and all that it stood for, its presence which dead-weighted her and the memories that corroborated it. The years of hunger. The rapes. The past infirmities that Sonoma suffered. The unthinkable.

"Well I should hope that you're Sonoma," Max said jovially, dressed in his usual formal attire, entering the yacht deck through an arched doorway. "Of course you are Sonoma," he said with a smile. "Who else would you be?" Max said as he straightened his black tie. "You're my Sonoma."

Immediately, Sonoma thrust back her hair to cover her neckline.

"Max, how did you get out here? When did you get back?" Sonoma smiled excitedly but meekly at the same time, embarrassed that Max had heard her utterance that she thought had been private.

"I didn't know you were there," Sonoma continued on

in nervousness, looking up at Max, then gazing at him, her heart fluttering like it always did when Max was around.

Max stopped and stared at Sonoma, playfully tilting his head for a moment with his usual chagrin. "I'm full of secrets," Max said smiling. "I wanted to surprise you. Did I?"

Sonoma was silent, her head bobbing above the water like an exotic creature of the sea. Sonoma sensed a slight difference in Max, something newly present in his ways.

"Sonoma, I know that look of yours," Max began. "You're going to Argentina, aren't you? You shouldn't be taking any trips, you know. Your schedule is booked."

Max had read Sonoma's mind, just like he had done so many times before.

Sonoma looked away at the horizon, the base line of her view. Sonoma had been dreaming about Argentina all week.

"I've been thinking about Argentina, that's all." Sonoma said.

Changing the subject, as if the accusation had ended, Max sat down at a covered glass table next to the ladder. The thick table glass was spotless and transparent, cool to touch, the six o'clock hot summer day starting to wind to the eve. The butlers appeared and quickly set the table, a dinner for two, they having ceremoniously performed the same for years.

"Sonoma, we've got to get back and get ready for tonight's book event," Max said to Sonoma, motioning to the captain as Sonoma climbed out of the water. "People will arrive at ten, the usual time."

Like a flower that blooms endlessly, Sonoma was still attractive, fit and healthy, a size six. Her dark blue eyes juxtaposed her pale skin, almost seeming at times that her eyes were aglow. Tall, blonde, and polished, Sonoma resembled an exotic flower, a rare find Max would often think to himself. Max had been a ladies' man in his previous years before he met Sonoma, never settling down with anyone and never wanting to, unbeknownst to Sonoma and not written in the mechanical, ritualistic days and years that they had shared together.

Sonoma slipped on a white robe and nestled into the chair next to Max. Toweling her long blonde hair, Sonoma's wet locks looked butterscotch in the shade, which Max loved. Why always so late and the same time?" Sonoma said to Max. "Why not schedule events differently?" Sonoma opined loosely and with ease.

"People are creatures of habit. Haven't you realized that yet?" Max said with a smile, reaching for a glass of ice water which he quietly gulped down briefly. "Besides," Max continued, "all great events begin in the dark. And your book-signing for your new book, 'How to Heal Within,' will be no different."

Sonoma shook her head smiling. "Well, whatever you say. That's why you take care of things."

"Yes, I do," Max said confidently and bluntly, while unlocking his briefcase. The briefcase popped open. Max pulled out his computer. "We've got to be prepared for tonight. I don't want any interference. Now let's go over again what you're going to say to Rodrigo when he arrives tonight. And we'll go through the others in the order we've practiced."

Astutely, though reluctantly, Sonoma went through the list with Max, pleasing him. The butlers watched Max and Sonoma from afar, sensing the happiness that exuded them as they naturally commingled, and in the simplest of ways. Spliced with pleasantries, charm, and kindness, Sonoma and Max always enjoyed their time together.

The two brought about a rare type of ignition that neither Sonoma nor Max had ever before felt and never would.

After returning to shore, Max left to attend to event details, he always orchestrating the buzz that precipitated the parties. Alone, Sonoma walked to the garden, the eight p.m. evening sun setting in the sky.

"My garden...my home," Sonoma said as she entered. Sonoma touched a bronze sign titled, "On Defining God," which hung visibly at the entrance. Of all the rooms and places in the mansion, the garden was Sonoma's favorite, a living sanctuary. Magnificent and superfluous, the garden took Sonoma's breath every time that she entered. A garden of all gardens, Sonoma had created it, the space now filled. Flowers and plants were everywhere. In decorative pots and containers, in the ground, in lily ponds, in playable marble harps, the plant life thrived in the space carefree. From peonies to tulips, to dandelions to roses, to flowery spinach plants to eggplants, the garden was lustrous, luscious, and vibrant, jam-packed abundantly with different colors, scents, and textures. Some were shipped from foreign lands, others were native to Miami. Sonoma delighted in the garden, planting each of them all and watching them grow, mature, and mingle. Sonoma had even created new plant varieties through hybrid breeding, but Sonoma refused to give them names, leaving the plants to define themselves. Max loved the garden too. Max sometimes went there by himself to marvel and spiritually bathe in the garden's beauty, always wondering how Sonoma's garden could continuously thrive, even with plants ill-zoned for the climate.

Laying down on a black iron settee, the sweet smell of flowers encompassed Sonoma, a symphony of them, melodic in arrangement and all sounding together.

Sonoma stared at the sky, watching the panoramic, glistening sunset evolve before her. Colors collaged together, color palates in motion, moving in sync with Sonoma's garden, her flowers looking up at the heavens too, drenched in heaven's silent song. Yellow, purple, and orange, separate but then merged, a unique painting by God and his authorities which would never be redrawn.

And as the sun set, Sonoma felt like a flower growing in the garden too, enriched by the soil, charged by the sun. Sonoma breathed the evening air, in and out, thinking of her life. The wealth that she had acquired, the fertility of her surroundings. The fame, the success, and the mysteries within them. The mansion, layers upon layers, rooms upon rooms, the mansion within her. The future possibilities. And Max, always in her mind's eye of the future, whom she loved deeply and with completeness, if only he knew, and she thought that he did.

CHAPTER 19

"Get out!" a woman screamed at the top of her lungs, glaring at her husband in rage, her eyes wide open with anger. Her long mink coat, non-Miami attire, tightened bristly like a porcupine, its rough texture ill-oiled and assaultive like her chaffed, dry red lips.

Sonoma heard the woman's ravenous scream amidst the soft violin music that played gently in the background. Sonoma was standing by herself in the back of the event room, a location unusual for Sonoma to stand during the events.

Sonoma froze, perplexed, wondering what would happen, what the woman would do, and why she was doing it. After all, Sonoma had attended numerous of these same book events, the same song and dance consistently transpiring, the same routine almost as rote and predictable as the rise of the sun and fall of the moon.

It was 11:00 p.m., one hour having passed since the book event began, and by all accounts the event had resembled the prior ones. A mock gold colored veranda, positioned prominently in the room's center, flickered with lit candles and sparkly gold ribbons, featuring Sonoma's books and including her latest one, "How to Heal Within." Max hosted the event and greeted the guests, supervising staff and assistants, the event going smoothly and methodically just like he'd planned. Stately and subdued, the pomp of the atmosphere had thickened like gravy, the usual 11:00 p.m. dense energy filling the palatial event room just like it had done so many times before and without incident.

In awe of the moment, the disparity of the present, Sonoma's eyes glued to the screaming woman. The woman's long finger pointed at her husband like a sword, a dagger on his life, her nails sharp like scissors only an inch from his eyes.

Instantly, like a window of time opened, Sonoma knew the story underlying the couple, both in context and color. Sonoma wondered, how do I know this? The woman had caught her husband cheating, once again, by staring slinkily upon another woman across the room. The other woman had smiled back. A forbidden exchange had been made between them.

"You monster!" the man screamed back to the woman. "You don't deserve to live! Why do you constantly slay me!" The man's words reverberated through the hall with strong vibrations.

With a loud thud, the man then thrust his wife's arm high into the air. The woman's hand and fingers slammed back against the wall behind her, crushing two of her fingers with his single force. The man then grabbed his wife by the head. He then bashed her head violently into the wall.

Sonoma watched in horror, paralyzed in disbelief at the events that were unfolding before her eyes.

Disfigured wall plaster fragments were everywhere. In the floor, on people's clothes, on people's faces, in their eyebrows. The woman's shapeless mold was embedded into the wall, saturating the wall with memory and the wall's cracks within her.

Severely injured, if not dead, the woman's body then slowly inched down the mangled wall, covered in blood, collapsing like a slow melt. A streak of blood followed the woman's head as little-by-little she edged downward, and then downward, then falling onto the floor. The event party's subdued ambience was unphased, without interruption, which was staggering to Sonoma's mind.

Still frozen in shock, Sonoma watched staff members run to the fallen lady. Stammering over her, her body lifeless, modes of activity ensuing. CPR took place, screams to call 911, the activities were multiple. Chaos wove around the fallen lady like a cocoon, despite the unchanged ambience that the guests were enjoying and creating.

Finally feeling the reality in the moment, Sonoma ran over to the injured woman. Staff members huddled around the lady like an impassable fortress of protection.

The ambiance then changed.

The violin music in the background lost its simmer, its notes boldly increasing in loudness and vitality. Within seconds, the violin's decibels raged, its notes screaming in the room like a flightless airplane had reached its destination from the beginning.

"Is she still alive?" Sonoma belted out loudly, her voice barely audible.

A female staff member turned and looked at Sonoma with confusion, plight marked on her face.

The chaos continued, Sonoma getting no answer. People were running around in front of the huddle blockading the injured woman. Sonoma felt claustrophobic. People crowded in all around Sonoma purportedly tending to the bloody woman. People were packed together tightly all around Sonoma, the air sealing in all around her, Sonoma barely able to breathe.

Then the bizarre…

Like time stood still, Sonoma looked to her left, feeling a bubble of silence in the crazed, monumentally moving room. Sonoma saw the husband, the assaulter…the one who had struck his wife and caused the damage and chaos. Sonoma saw his face, which was paralyzed in fear. Sonoma saw his hands trembling in trepidation. His hands were covered in his wife's blood, the tension striving to escape as his body repeatedly shook, blood dripping from his hands and onto the floor.

The man didn't mean to kill his wife. Sonoma felt the message coming from his soul. Sonoma closed her eyes. Sonoma could feel and hear the words in her mind, all of the emotions and feelings that the man was feeling. Sonoma could feel the man's remorse and the sediment already forming within him by the erosion of his deceased wife that had now passed.

Then all of a sudden, amidst the confusion and trauma, the female staff member turned to Sonoma. "She's fine, Ms. Lively. She's just dancing." The staff member looked aloof and nonchalant and casually nodded to Sonoma after her words were complete, like her words didn't match her movements, being out of sync. Sonoma was mystified at the words, not registering them, they being completely nonsensical words for the moment, like the staff member was seeing another world unfold, not the scene that Sonoma was viewing.

The staff member then scurried off and disappeared into the contours of the room.

So did the crowds. The frenzied groups suddenly dispersed and without reason, went back to their own ways in the event room like the assault upon the woman had never happened.

Sonoma glanced back in front of her, with jolt and half vision.

The music was soft again. The violin was gently playing. It was like the violinist was playing its instrument to rock a baby to sleep. It's strings sounded softly and with a fresh free flow of its notes, the complete opposite of what Sonoma had just witnessed moments before.

Sonoma looked around, still standing in the place where the huddled people had blocked her. Still standing where she had seen the bloody scene unravel, and the man unravel too.

The woman's blood was gone. It had vanished. Not a drop of blood was on the floor. The event room wall was intact. Perfectly plastered, smooth and shiny, no destruction was apparent of any kind.

In front of Sonoma was the woman who had been bludgeoned. Again, tightly coiled in her mink coat, the woman was chatting and gossiping loudly to other women, the lady's eyes following her husband with precision across the room and calculating his every move.

Sonoma stood there dazed. What had just happened? Sonoma's thoughts raced through her mind.

Sonoma was trying to understand the scenes that she had just witnessed, that were now gone. Sonoma's thoughts barraged her, fighting each other. Was the vision real? Was it a premonition? Why were maddening sights and impressions appearing, and more often?

Max studied Sonoma from across the room, just as he'd done systematically for years. Max sensed a difference imminent in Sonoma. He could feel it from

Sonoma's eyes and the way that she held her hands, an essence pivoting in Sonoma's ways and movements and most of all, in Sonoma's vantage point.

"The transition," Max said as he took a drink of red wine from his glass.

Like the tide, Sonoma's perception was changing. Realms were showing themselves, and including what they had been and what they were. Sonoma's vision was strengthening with acuity and focus. It was only a matter of time.

Max sensed Sonoma's discomfort in the process. Max remembered his own past when he went through the same trials. Max wished that he could help Sonoma, if only he could. Max's palms were sweaty and hot with anxiety, drip gathering on his forehead. Max dried his hands in his pockets. Max knew that the transition was happening, that Sonoma was close to putting the pieces together. Connecting the dots of the picture that already exists, and herself the only instrument that could unite them.

Suddenly, like time froze, Sonoma felt the momentum in the moment.

Sonoma gazed fully around the room, mammoth in size. Sonoma listened acutely, her eyes configuring the vast space. Seeing the activity within it, Sonoma felt and touched the room and guests with her eyes. Calculating slowly and with measure, one breath at a time.

All around her, fans and media catwalked the marbleized floor. One lady walked by with a bright pink umbrella, 1950's style, frilled on the ends like in old movies that Sonoma had seen. The lady's bleached blonde hair was as bright as her umbrella. The lady strolled around the room like she owned it, the umbrella her microphone as she chatted and danced.

A married couple dressed alike, both in tuxedos, white paint on their faces, walked by in delight. The two were in a comedy play about the struggles of marriage, which they informed everyone around. The couple laughed hysterically in the room, enjoying their walk, genuine love in their eyes, not for each other but for the stable images that they portrayed.

People drank wine and ate fancy foods, conversing with each other. A low buzz moved through the room as people connected their voices and proximity, hand movements flowing loosely like the moments that passed. Women were wearing floral wrist corsages, and flowers were pinned to men's suits. Sonoma recognized the flowers, her flowers, all freshly cut from her garden, "On Defining God."

Instantly, and with strike, a realization came over Sonoma. "How could I have missed it?" Sonoma said as she gazed around the room.

The patterns, the patterns of her guests. Sonoma had seen them before.

The same guests, all of them, at her other book events.

Minutes went by. Sonoma continued studying the patterns, recognizing other guests, and then more guests, like she was watching a movie that she had already seen.

Sonoma stood there alone in the back of the room engulfed in the moment. Sonoma banished all other thoughts, familiarity soaking within her.

With a corresponding flash, Sonoma's thought then dissipated, rationalization entering. Crazed insurgents, Sonoma reasoned. People who repeatedly attended her events searching for meaning, constantly and ongoingly critiquing her works, intrusive to Sonoma in every way. Sonoma then meandered around the room with an oddly relaxed, outgoing energy, unlike Sonoma's usual stationary, guarded approach. Max watched Sonoma closely, her exuding seamless, effortless navigation as she handled the crowds like fragile instruments while playing them.

With control surrendered, Max noticed Sonoma mutter trite, hollow words to her guests and fluidly, devoid of pre-conceived intention or thought. The template alive, conversations then erupted and other exchanges followed, like energy pockets opening in the room, unique sculpted bubbles template-borne in small grouped tepees of people huddled intermittently throughout the room.

Max watched with nervous delight. Max reveled in the relaxed, grounded patterns that were emerging within Sonoma which he could see with his eyes. It was an evolution that Max had waited for so long, yearned for so long, his anticipation high.

Max approached Sonoma in a small crowd, politely breaking her away for a brief word on the balcony. The ocean below, the stars in the sky, the outside air silkened the celebratory mood.

"You're different tonight," Max said to Sonoma while gently touching her shoulder.

"I am," Sonoma said confidently, smiling.

Sonoma stared into Max's deep blue eyes, his warm hands warming her skin as the soft breeze blew through her hair.

"It's like you're out of your shell," Max said, and with a pause.

Sonoma smiled in reassurance. "I feel more myself," Sonoma said gracefully, staring out into the vast ocean, the waves caressing the sand below them.

After a long pause between them, Max turned and grabbed hold of the balcony rail. Sonoma was close in front of him. Max was facing Sonoma, their bodies only five inches apart. Max felt Sonoma's energy, so strong yet so fragile. Pivoting and changing, Max could feel Sonoma's energy swirling, like a heartbeat climbing to another tempo, discovering new currents, new directions of travel. Sonoma's yellow dress swayed back and forth in the evening air, following the lead of the wind.

"You're going, aren't you," Max said bluntly to Sonoma. "You're going to Argentina. I can feel it. I know."

Sonoma looked away with a slight smile. Sonoma's silent charisma was as bright as the yellow dress that she wore. "You know me, don't you," Sonoma said with a grin.

And Max did, and Sonoma knew that he did.

Suddenly, with brazen, a giant of a man named Asaro Rodrigo approached Sonoma on the balcony. He was seven foot tall and dressed in formal military attire. The middle-aged man showcased his large frame by his shirt full of military pins and ribbons. Symbolic accomplishments were stuck to him, a walking pin-board of pain. Rodrigo was the man that Max had warned Sonoma about and prepared her to meet.

A fifty year old billionaire from Venezuela, Rodrigo had made his fortune in the oil industry. He had ten or more wives, women who toured with him country-to-country, always clamoring over him silently like he was a spoiled child being kept. Max had met Rodrigo in Europe. Rodrigo had demanded to meet with Sonoma, and Max had negotiated the terms. According to Max, Rodrigo was an avid reader and writer, seeking to change the world with dictatorship and own everything in sight. A self-proclaimed teacher and leader, Rodrigo had dispersed and marketed his teachings all over the world, his focus now on the United States to gain notoriety and fame.

"Well, Max McCallister..." Rodrigo bellowed out in a slow, scratchy voice filled with obtuseness, acknowledging Max and Sonoma while making his presence known. "I'm finally here. Weren't you expecting me?" Rodrigo then laughed deeply and darkly, sinister tones sounding, like his inside matched his outside, full of piercing, sharp pins.

Max politely greeted Rodrigo and then excused himself from the veranda. Rodrigo acknowledged Max's cue, for the private meeting with Sonoma that Rodrigo had requested.

Alone with Rodrigo on the balcony, Sonoma was prepared to answer his questions just like she and Max had rehearsed. Sonoma stood there comfortably, at ease, mentally perusing the manufactured bullet points in her mind.

Rodrigo scanned Sonoma's body, beginning with Sonoma's strapless yellow dress and descending down Sonoma's body like a burglar in the night.

Sonoma opened her mouth, ready to be unleash. To address Rodrigo once and for all, just like she'd planned.

Suddenly, Rodrigo violently thrust his arm around Sonoma's neck, grabbing the bones of her neck tightly and with force. Rodrigo's giant arm obstructed Sonoma's airway, blockading her oxygen. A death grip, strangling her, Sonoma could feel her oxygen running out. Stifled, petrified in panic, Rodrigo's mouth then engulfed her lips in a ravaging kiss, his pulsating breath audible.

"What are you doing!" Sonoma screamed with rage, ferociously jumping back away from Rodrigo, struggling for air, repulsed at his attack and unfathomable actions.

Sonoma's backwards move drove Rodrigo's fingernails

into her skin, carving a blood drawn scratch from the top of her neck to her chest and slicing her silk dress.

Rodrigo was pacified in delight. Rodrigo had accomplished the purpose of the meeting. His wounds were now imprinted upon Sonoma, exactly as he had wanted.

Rodrigo growled, his voice animalistic. Rodrigo's face then morphed into a monster that Sonoma hadn't seen since she was a child at Café Piraza. Rodrigo chided Sonoma in a grisly, venom-filled voice, "You are delusional, Ms. Lively."

Blood trickled down Sonoma's chest. Sonoma's yellow silk dress soaked up the falling blood, embracing the blood with its fibers.

Sonoma screamed a tormenting wail, running from the balcony to the event room in cataclysmic fear. "Max!"

Max appeared almost immediately.

"Rodrigo attacked me!" Sonoma said in anguish. "He strangled me! I have blood and it…"

Sonoma looked down at her dress, stopping in mid-sentence.

No blood was on Sonoma's dress. There were no signs of attack. No blood. No wound. No blood, Sonoma thought again. Sonoma looked down at her yellow dress, perfectly unharmed. The illusions were overwhelming. The images were real. Sonoma was again drowned in disbelief at the scenes that she had just witnessed, though banishing rationalization this time.

Sonoma stood there speechless, ready to fall, collapse into anywhere but the scene that embraced her.

Max grabbed Sonoma's hand. Max kissed Sonoma's forehead as she stood motionless and quiet. Max held Sonoma tight with his arms, securing her with his body.

Wearing his usual jagged edge, Rodrigo came out from

the balcony to where Max and Sonoma were standing. Rodrigo's face was splotchy and red. Veins protruded out of his forehead like frayed wires.

"I travelled 2,000 miles to have my say to you, Ms. Lively, and I will have it."

Sonoma took a deep breath.

"You walking away won't deter me," Rodrigo continued. "I am a rich man, and I didn't make my fortune giving it away. Or, encouraging people to use their own power. To be successful in this world, you must take what you deserve by force. It's fundamental to success and growth, which all of your charity books contradict. I am here to warn you. Beware, you false prophet! If you continue your books, then I'll burn every one of them, and you too. You will write your own death!"

Rodrigo then abruptly turned and left, rage burning visibly within him. Rodrigo's entourage of wives and security trailed behind like empty, clanging tin cans on a string.

Then at precisely 12:00 a.m., just like the other countless book events before, the party ended. As guests left, their eyes traced back to Sonoma as they departed. A lady waved to Sonoma as she exited the hall door. Sonoma recognized the lady but couldn't pinpoint from where. The lady had long brown hair, dark eyes, and a scar on her forehead. Max's arms were still enveloping Sonoma as staff peripherally brought the event to a close.

By 2:00 a.m., Sonoma's private plane was in the air for Argentina. Sonoma didn't say goodbye to Max when she left, and she regretted it. Goodbye was hard to say. Goodbye was all that Sonoma had ever known as a child.

A fourteen hour flight, Sonoma sat alone with dimmed lights peering out of the window, thinking about him, her

Max, and his strong arms around her amidst the dazzling, bizarre confusion that Sonoma had seen and felt. Of Max's sweet kiss on her forehead and what it meant to her, and what it might have meant to him. Of Max's comforting voice that seemed to extricate fear out of Sonoma like pages being torn from a book and placed out into the open for Sonoma to see, illusions no more.

With only darkness in sight, Sonoma rested comfortably holding her thoughts, as the Challengers plane held her, taking Sonoma to her planned destination.

CHAPTER 20

The tepid dark air accosted Sonoma as she made her way through the deplane zone. Sonoma had been awake most of the fourteen hour flight, unable to sleep, sitting by herself in the back of the plane while Challengers staff members occupied the front.

A rustic cobblestone pathway lead Sonoma to the airport terminal entrance. Sonoma examined the stones as she made her way down the path, already bringing back memories. The staff followed obediently behind Sonoma carrying her luggage and belongings. They looked like military soldiers marching together in the early morning night. Some were half-sleep, others awake, all muted as they walked.

It had been over thirteen years since Sonoma had last been to Argentina, and then only for a few days when Max had found Aubella in foster care. There were cracks in Max's story as to how he had found Aubella and at precisely the same time that Sonoma had arrived in Argentina. For years, Sonoma had tried to get the whole story from Max, repeatedly. Each time, Max would say that the foster parents didn't know Aubella's background, and that he found her by chance. Max said that the foster parents had died, and that their full names now escaped him. Sonoma obsessed about the omissions of Aubella's story, and including where Aubella had been living and with whom for those shrouded five years and what happened to Mother Agnes.

Sonoma entered the terminal and went through customs. Sonoma instructed her staff to go on to the hotel, that she had arranged for separate transportation. Sonoma said that she had business to do and that they'd convene at noon. Confused and dazed at any sort of business at the hour, the staff nonetheless complied, going on to the hotel with the baggage, it rolling tiredly behind them.

"Hotel Bleu," Sonoma shouted to the staff, "that's where you're staying!" The staff motioned back to Sonoma, acknowledging her directive while they continued their blind walk to the shuttle.

After the staff was gone, Sonoma motioned a random cab driver for service.

A yellow cab pulled up. Its yellow paint was disheveled and blotched with rust.

The cab driver rolled down his window. "Where to?" the elderly man said alertly to Sonoma, his Argentinean accent beautiful, music to Sonoma's ears. The man wore a gold coin necklace, shiny and bright.

"Café Pariza," Sonoma said in her own corresponding Argentinean accent. Immediately, the driver knew that Sonoma was native to Argentina despite her contrary Miami dress and style.

Sonoma felt safe with the driver. His mature appearance soothed Sonoma's nerves. He looked to be about seventy years old with wrinkles all over his face and neck. His sun splotched hands were also tattered and worn, like the inside of a used baseball mitt on a hot summer day.

Sonoma knew that the man's wisdom was guiding her.

The cab driver was silent, his eyes wide, as he silently loaded Sonoma's belongings into the back trunk. He would take Sonoma to the requested destination, though he strove to avoid Café Piraza and the roads that surrounded it. The driver had been there before.

The car ride was silent. Café Piraza was thirty minutes away. Exhausted, Sonoma rested in the gashes of the torn leather seat gazing out the window as the cab moved along. The inside of the cab smelled like shoe polish and male cologne, bringing back memories of her life as a child at Café Piraza when men lined the halls.

Sonoma tried to think of something else. Looking out of the window, Sonoma watched blackened houses sprinkled in the darkness around her periodically awaken and come to life. Like muted fireworks in the night, house lights turned on, its sleepers having risen, people beginning their new day. Sonoma imagined what it would be like to awaken each day with a lover, a spouse. To begin each new day with them, a companion bonded for life. Sonoma thought of Max, sweet Max, so kind, dedicated, and caring. Sonoma wondered what he was doing and if he were thinking of her.

Soon, Sonoma arrived at the location of Café Pariza. The cab driver slowly rolled to a stop in front of the private drive leading to Café Piraza. It was clear that the driver intentionally stopped his travel short, not wanting to travel the remaining distance to the main Café Piraza building.

"Too bumpy," the man said in his eloquent Argentinean accent. The man hunkered his head down low, pointing to the private drive. He put the car's headlights on high beam, to help Sonoma navigate her way.

Sonoma asked the cab driver to wait for her, that she wouldn't be long.

The cab driver nodded, saying nothing as he cranked down the window and turned off the engine. The headlights illuminated the private drive as Sonoma exited the car.

When Sonoma's feet touched the private drive, the driver's radio turned on. An odd station played what sounded to be 1800's music, emanating from the cab like a dissipating scent as Sonoma headed down the drive.

Alone and in the moonlight, Sonoma walked cautiously down the severely steep - but then inclined - path of cobblestones. Like the land was confused in its making, whether up or down, Sonoma felt the land's confusion, its juxtaposition, in her walk.

The cobblestone pathway tosselled Sonoma back and forth as she walked. Many parts were balded with pebbled debris. Other parts were full of cobblestones and in perfect alignment. Overgrown trees pervaded the pathway, the trees puffed up like bullies and guards exerting its authority over its walkers.

Sonoma was afraid. Afraid not of walking the path, but reaching the end of it and seeing what she had always feared. It had been so many years since Sonoma had been to Café Piraza, since Sonoma was sixteen years old that late September night.

Sonoma thought of the many times that she had been stolen in the night, Thefts - missing parts of her soul - that had been shattered there. The parts that were now beckoning her back. Catalysts for her writing…for her career…for her work, and most of all, for her beloved

Aubella. The parts that were now calling Sonoma to come back home.

Acknowledging the fear, but continuing to walk, Sonoma reached the top of the private drive.

And there, the moonlight shining upon it, enchantingly bright, was Café Piraza. The building looked just like Sonoma remembered. Sonoma had missed Café Piraza, though she hated it, the place where she had grown up as a child too quickly before her years.

"I am here," Sonoma whispered to Café Piraza.

Sonoma felt a calm cover her body from head-to-toe.

Sonoma gazed upon the corpse of the building, its dilapidated state, but sensing that it still had a pulse of its own.

The building whispered back. Not in human words but humane ones: words which Sonoma understood the meaning of with senses higher than the five. Like how Sonoma feels when a tree trembles before a storm, the way the tree communicates its temperament by rustling wind through its wings, its branches. Or, how Sonoma feels when fluxing wind self-gauges its flight like invisible birds swooshing in all around her in mischievousness in the open air. The wind expressing its vitality through creative play, the children of the sky. Or, how Sonoma feels when she sees the colors of a rainbow in its demi circle design. A silk-screen in the making, appearing then disappearing, articulating that nothing lasts forever and that collapse is a certainty and the first step of rebirth. Communicating that a new canvas will come, and with retracement from the last, and that more rainbows will arise, a certainty too. A telepathic cornucopia of energies, making themselves known through their language, fluency enjoyed by all once they are stilled.

Sonoma saw the windows of the building wink at her,

happy to see her home. It was their way of saying welcome, their eyes gazing upon her in a sneaking fashion so that the building's monsters wouldn't hear them. The windows then periodically creaked, again their way of welcoming Sonoma, its lost child, that they never forgot.

Café Piraza looked exactly as Sonoma remembered. Ancient and dilapidated, the massive gray rock and wooden boarding house stood solid before Sonoma, asserting its powerful structure and force just as it had done all those many years before. On the front door, which Sonoma had travelled through thousands of times, was the same jagged sign "Café Pariza" still hanging, just like in her memories and the diner newspaper all those years ago.

Café Piraza was enormous. It contained over forty rooms. In the middle of Café Piraza was the main homestead and school. Overgrown shrubbery fluffily encircled it, shrouding its face from the world. The main house is where Sonoma and the other children had lived, essentially by themselves. Eight children would sleep in one room, always sleeping on the floor. The children's rooms were always quiet, despite each room's multiple occupancy.

To the left and right of the main homestead were separate wings of twenty rooms. The state had ordered that the orphaned children live in the winged rooms. Ebetrio, however, had other plans. When Ebetrio took over as school master, he converted them to other use.

Startled for a moment, like a lightning bolt, Sonoma realized that she hadn't been in all of the rooms. No history, no stories there, Sonoma thought. The partial vacancy felt strange to Sonoma since Café Piraza had imprisoned her for sixteen years.

Sonoma thought of the many rooms, however, that

she had been in and the trauma of each stay, recorded by her eyes without any means to escape.

Café Piraza's wings, like the main headquarters, looked angry and sad at the same time, and in blended degrees. Chipped rocks in the building frowned upon Sonoma. Wood splinters warned her not to come close, else be pierced. Old rusty nails stuck out of wooden planks sporadically, aiming to stab any passerby that unfortunately passed its way.

But amidst the building's anger, a flagrant sadness pervaded the building which Sonoma recognized now more than ever before. It was in the way that the building was standing, how it slightly leaned to one side. Like it was tired of holding it all together and was ready to fall.

Perhaps the wild grasses would soften the building's fall, when that day finally came, Sonoma thought. Behind Café Piraza sprawled the tall pasture. Its wild grasses were untamed, exactly like Sonoma remembered. Beautifully unkempt and uncombed, the pasture embodied the perfect unshackled life.

"I love you," Sonoma whispered to the pasture.

Despite the fear, anger, angst, and desperation that Sonoma felt standing in front of Café Piraza, shreds of unexplainable happiness filled Sonoma's heart. Not at what happened, the past, the years of abuse. Or the terror, the brutality, the rapes and the killings. But of the connection: the her then to the her now. The connection that albeit the wreckage of Sonoma's past, she was here in this moment, this now, memorialized in time.

With a deep sigh and pause, Sonoma turned around and there, like years before, was the bench. "The bench," Sonoma whispered, amazed and delighted at its presence, a re-lived excitement unfolding within her that she had experienced as a child.

Severely worn, parts of the bench were missing. Chunks of it, cracks everywhere, though its concrete foundation was sturdy and solid.

Sonoma sat down on the bench, losing her breath for a moment. Sonoma's legs embraced the bench that had always supported her. The bench knew that Sonoma was there. It had been waiting for her. Sonoma cherished the bench and all the goodness that it had brought her. Never did Sonoma imagine, however, that the bench would still be there, the concrete bench that Sonoma had played on as a child. Where each day Sonoma would sit and dream, staring at the sky, wondering what lay outside of the horizon which boxed her in. Where Sonoma would bring her few toys and they would magically spring to life, their sweet ragged doll faces which Sonoma remembered with exactness. Sonoma's friends, her companions, the toys quiet though talking to her more than anyone ever did, a place of family and fellowship, the bench a sanctuary of worship, to live and let live, the bench's happiness and joy drowning out the monsters before it.

Staring out from the bench, Sonoma noticed the large oak tree in front of her. A towering tree that had always masked the front door, its leaves were full and thick, both in summer and winter, never shedding its leaves like its normal breed. The tree's thick, healthy limbs hung low upon the ground, ready to scoop Sonoma up and take her for a ride.

With a twinkle, Sonoma noticed a wooden box lodged up against the tree's giant trunk. Like the wooden box was bolstering the tree's angle, giving it direction, pointing it to the heavens by its pressing force.

Sonoma walked over to the tree. The wooden box

was long and wide with etched markings in its grain. Its circular wood rings looked like carvings, its markings betelling its ancient age. Cold, rusty metal hinges bound the top of the box shut, unlocked. A wooden casket for the living as it lay there above-ground.

Sonoma opened the box.

The first item that Sonoma saw was a picture frame. Placed in the center of the box, Sonoma felt its beg for attention. The moonlight brilliant all around her, Sonoma picked up the picture and blew the dust from the glass, the encased, glass image revealing itself.

It was her, Sonoma, as a young child, five years old. The same girl that Sonoma had seen in the ocean and wearing the same clothes. Its metal frame was corroded and coppery, like a battery had spilled.

Sonoma touched the girl's face in the picture, knowing that the smile was an illusion. Where did the girl go…Sonoma thought with tranquility.

Sonoma traced the girl's profile with her finger. So many years had passed.

Sonoma remembered the day that the photo had been taken, including the very second that it had been snapped. Sonoma had been so proud to be photographed, to be replicated by art. Sonoma remembered the visitor at Café Piraza aiming the camera at her, and then a flash lighting up the room. And for that brief moment, Sonoma felt worthy to be alive…to be art, and in the presence of art. Sonoma knew at a young age that the camera was man-made eyes, the photographer as much art as the pictures that he captured, the lenses changeable at his fingertips.

Sonoma then noticed a flashlight. Her flashlight, contraband as Café Piraza called it. It was the flashlight that Sonoma would steal from Café Piraza's tool room every night when she would climb out of the bedroom window and head for the field. Army green, the flashlight was roughed up and scratched, inoperable she was sure though it served its mission faithfully for Sonoma when she needed it all those years. It provided light in the darkness amidst the thick pastures that Sonoma walked. Sonoma was always searching for a secret village hidden in the tall grasses or a witch in the jungle, a good witch of course. The flashlight had secret powers that God had enthroned. It would make evil disappear by transforming evil into good - purple doves - which would then fly away to live on a happiness-filled distant island.

The flashlight was like a sword with no puncture, but with all the protection. Every night, the flashlight lit Sonoma's way to foreign worlds and lands, the topography uncharted by any other journeyman or discoverer.

Then the belt, a guillotine to Sonoma. Sonoma saw the leather belt in the box, curled up like a snake ready to strike, just as it had done so many times to Sonoma's skin as a child. Sonoma remembered the sounds of the leather belt machine. Mechanical thrusts of pain, an instrument that its recipients did not want to hear. Between lashes, the belt took breaths of its own, each breath longer than the last as the belt stung and violated her like a thousand bees. Unlike the other items, the belt was perfectly intact. It looked like the belt had never been used, its leather unchaffed despite its memory-recorded briar-filled compilations of swipes.

Sonoma unraveled the belt. Its metal loop and notch clanged together on the ground, mocking Sonoma's attempt to control it.

It was the belt of Ebetrio.

Sonoma knew every inch of it. The one that Ebetrio wore daily and used daily as he, the unbeatable, inflicted wounds upon the children of Café Piraza and including her.

Sonoma wondered if the items should be buried, like the dead.

Sonoma then thought of that late September night.

And with the daylight approaching, the new day being birthed, Sonoma put the items in her arms and returned to the bench, gazing up into the moonlit sky.

The heavy moon bowed to Sonoma, and with a shimmer of purple, like amethyst, that Sonoma could see...really see. A flashlight of all flashlights, Sonoma stared at the bright, radiant moon, her compass, showing her the way.

"Where the purple doves fly," Sonoma said with a newfound understanding.

CHAPTER 21

"It's time, Ms. Lively," the young male assistant said nervously to Sonoma, helping Sonoma out of the hotel and onto the loading deck.

Sonoma sensed and felt the young man's uneasiness, like he was carrying bricks on his back.

"Sonoma... Call me Sonoma," Sonoma replied graciously. Sonoma then extended her hand out to him.

The young man shook her hand politely, stress falling from his shoulders. The young man's youth contrasted sharply with his mature manners. Sonoma surmised that he couldn't be more than eighteen years old.

"Sonoma...," the young man restated in front of her with a gentle smile. Sonoma sensed courage in his tone, she recognizing the sweet sound of it.

"It is a blessing to have you here," Sonoma said with vibrance, making any hint of awkwardness disappear. "This is a big day for me."

For years, Sonoma had dreamt of this day. Every night after being moved to Miami, Sonoma would ponder this day and with varying measures of hope. What she would do, how she would do it. What the day would hold, and how it would happen. In all the many years of counseling at the Challengers, the most effective tool for Sonoma had been her dreams, her ponderings, the plans that Sonoma had built in the sky at night, blueprints that evolved over time as she aged, for that certain day, this day, the day of confrontation.

Sonoma reached for her briefcase. It was large, two feet in width. The briefcase was made out of black snakeskin and was shiny, like a freshly minted and polished coin. The top clasps of it were made out of gold, and the sides bore bronze and silver delicate chains, dangling loosely but with structure.

The briefcase was like Sonoma, both formal and casual depending on the view. It was the first costly item that Sonoma had ever purchased. She had bought it on a mission in Paris after Sonoma had written her first book. A day that Sonoma had earmarked with joy, the briefcase was a symbol of new beginning for Sonoma. Sonoma had shed her skin.

Grabbing the soft handles of the briefcase, Sonoma felt the smooth snakeskin divisions in the grip of her fingers. The divisions felt like a map, each imprint a separate country, all living together but separated by the map maker's drawn boundaries.

"Do you want me to carry that for you?" the young male assistant offered Sonoma regarding Sonoma's briefcase.

"Oh no," Sonoma laughed. "I've got it. Thank you." The day was an important walk for Sonoma, one that Sonoma would make herself.

Sonoma carried the black briefcase down to the hotel shuttle, loading for Café Piraza. Again, Sonoma signaled for the staff to go on, that she had other transportation.

The staff acquiesced, leaving Sonoma behind. Sonoma had arranged for the same cab driver to transport her the rest of the trip. His few words made Sonoma feel safe and secure, comfort that Sonoma needed for the day and the days ahead.

The drive to Café Piraza in the bright daylight was much different than the early morning trip. The daylight revealed the region's poverty, its cape of concealing darkness gone. People sat hopelessly in their yards, staring out from rusty chairs with sunken, vacant eyes, cloaked with hunger, which Sonoma recognized. Impoverished people walked barefoot on the crackled, broken road, its pavement in as much disrepair as the houses which they led to. Many houses had been abandoned, repair too costly or impossible to give them another life.

The distance seemed longer. The roads felt rougher. The air felt thicker, like a smog was covering them and had attached to them, impeding their travel. Giant potholes and bumps threw Sonoma around in the car, displacements that Sonoma didn't recall from the early morning hours. Sonoma wondered if the cab driver were taking a different route to Café Piraza, which he was not.

Sonoma was appalled at the poverty which she was passing. Appalled not only because Sonoma was passing it without stopping to help, but also because she had seen it so many times as a child and like a trigger, the experience of poverty began emerging from her soul. Hunger pains... Pains of poverty... Sonoma breathed deeply, inhaling and exhaling, just like she had practiced in therapy for years and privately with Max too.

The cab driver looked back at Sonoma every once and a while during the car ride.

Sonoma and her staff were expected at Café Piraza at

10:00 a.m., the time of the first meeting. Arranging the meeting had been difficult. Sonoma's staff had worked on the meeting for a week, the same week that Max had been gone. From phone calls, to detectives, to contact with the town's mayor, to contact with the police and other government authorities, many different resources had been utilized to arrange the meeting.

The cab arrived at Café Piraza. The hotel shuttle was in front of the cab, looking like a small train and the cab it's caboose.

Unlike the morning, the cab driver didn't stop in front of the private drive to Café Piraza. Instead, the cab driver followed the shuttle's lead, turning onto the private drive and driving slowly deeply down - and then skycrapingly up - its polarized path. The cab jostled back and forth from the rough, jarring cobblestone driveway.

The cab finally came to a grating stop. Smoke billowed out from underneath the cab and the shuttle, both coughing and panting from the rough roadway just travelled.

Getting out of their vehicles, Sonoma and her staff stood in front of Café Piraza in silence. Sonoma could feel that they felt uneasy about Café Piraza's presence before them. Like Sonoma, they could feel the evil in Café Piraza, the demons who lived there and the ones who wanted to, dark energies in Café Piraza.

Taking the lead, her briefcase in hand, Sonoma climbed up Café Piraza's steps and onto the porch. The wood floor absorbed the steps of Sonoma's confident, affirmative walk.

Sonoma knocked on the door, holding her briefcase with one hand. The staff members moved in behind Sonoma.

"Café Piraza," Sonoma said with determination.

Sonoma shook her head in disgust at the jagged sign on the door.

A local realtor answered the door, opening it wide. It was the lady that Sonoma's staff had worked with via telephone for the week.

"Ms. Lively, it's so wonderful to meet you," the realtor said professionally and politely.

"A pleasure," Sonoma responded, shaking her hand.

The realtor led Sonoma and her staff into a parlor. Sonoma recognized the parlor instantly, memories flooding her mind. The parlor was filled with antique lime green furniture and items, matching its lime green crackled walls. Sonoma recognized the room's contents and including a chipped blue water pitcher sitting on a wooden stand next to the couch.

"So here we are, Ms. Lively. This is your house now. I'm thrilled that you purchased it. It'd been sitting empty for so many years. It needs some repair, but you know that. I'm shocked that you closed on this real estate in one week. I guess it pays to be rich."

Sonoma was shocked at the woman's words.

"Thank you," Sonoma responded.

Sonoma looked around for a few moments, silently acclimating to the room.

"I assume that you'll give me the keys and paperwork. My attorney said that you'd have it for me."

"Oh yes," the realtor responded while reaching into her purse. The realtor handed Sonoma the executed deed along with the keys, a giant silver key ring of them. The keys were the original barrel keys to Café Piraza and all of its rooms.

"One more thing," the realtor said to Sonoma. "The former housekeeper was hoping to meet with you. She says that she worked here for a long time."

Sonoma was surprised and taken back. Café Piraza had never had a housekeeper. The orphanage children were its housekeeper.

"I'll be glad to meet with her. When does she want to meet?" Sonoma said with composure.

"Today, I guess. She's here. The lady somehow found out about the meeting and showed up right before you got here. She's out back."

"No problem, Sonoma said loosely. "I'll be glad to meet with her."

"Well I'm done here. The building is yours. Good luck to you, Ms. Lively."

The meeting ended.

The realtor left.

Sonoma held the keys in disbelief. The dream of purchasing Café Piraza had materialized.

There was now only one more meeting for the day. The second meeting was set for noon. Sonoma prayed that the second meeting would go smoothly too.

With the legalities complete, Sonoma sent her staff back to the hotel until the next morning. Sonoma wanted to digest everything around her in private. The sights and the sounds, and the sights within the sounds, alone. Sonoma gave her staff no explanation for the continuance. Their acquiescence, however, while an order, told Sonoma that they knew.

Café Piraza was now quiet. Only Sonoma was in its dwelling.

Sonoma then remembered the woman on the porch.

Sonoma looked outside the kitchen window. A large, elderly woman was sitting on the patio steps, her back to the house. The woman was dressed in long black clothing, covering most of her body, like the attire of a catholic nun.

Sonoma opened the kitchen door and walked outside to greet her. "Maam... Hello," Sonoma said to the lady. Sonoma extended out her hand.

The woman slowly stood and turned around. Her face was rutted and dark.

"Name's Vivienno," the woman said to Sonoma. The woman disregarded Sonoma's hand, leaving it awkwardly in the air. Unmatched, ungreeted, connected only with disconnection.

Dispelling the awkward moment with intention, Sonoma's arm fell to her side. Sonoma struggled for words. "Come in," Sonoma said with hesitance, motioning the woman into the house.

The lady headed into the house. The lady sat down in the kitchen like she knew the room well, like she had sat in the chair before and was familiar with its contours.

Sonoma initiated the conversation, now recreating awkwardness with intention. "So why are you here? What do you want?"

The woman's short dark gray hair pulled back tightly from her hairline with rigidity and stress, her forehead driving it. The woman hastily impinged, "I don't want you buying Café Piraza. It's not for sale," she said with impunity. Her voice was unbalanced like her appearance, uncertainty written all over her.

The woman's words confused and perplexed Sonoma. Sonoma looked down and under the table, seeing the woman's shoes which were badly worn like her face.

"You can't own this house!" the woman yelled furiously at Sonoma. "I don't want you here!" The woman's dark brown eyes, almost black, stared holes through Sonoma.

Sonoma paused and collected herself.

"I don't want to be rude, but I own this place. I own

Café Piraza. It is my property now. Would you like to see the deed?"

Sonoma handed the woman the deed.

The woman threw the deed in the air, it landing behind her.

The woman's tone then lowered in energy, like a different person was speaking. "This is my home. I've been here for decades," the woman said softly and quietly.

"There is no way...," Sonoma said harshly. "I used to live here. If you lived here, then I would remember you. When were you here?"

The woman's scornful energy returned. "I'm warning you... You need to leave. This is not the place for you!"

Sonoma stood and pushed the chair back. "Get out! Leave! It's time for you to leave!"

The lady stood up irately and slammed her chair into the wall. The woman's wide hips dominated the room, like she was pitching a large black tent in the room to mark her territory.

Then the woman raised the bottom of her dress to her knees and shrieked out a loud, high pitched screech. The scream sounded non-human, like a crazed, bawling siren.

The woman then ran out of the kitchen door. The ill-hung screen door slammed shut like a mousetrap, parts of it vibrating with linger and without any form or pattern. The house echoed behind her, her vile sounds too much for it to absorb.

Sonoma ran to the door, frantically gazing out of its delicately crisscrossed metal.

The woman was gone. No woman was in sight.

Sonoma ran to the side door in the parlor. The woman was nowhere to be found. Sonoma then ran to the front door, and then outside of it and around the main entrance to Café Piraza. No woman... No sign of her presence. The woman was nowhere to be found.

Sonoma wondered how the woman could have left Café Piraza without Sonoma seeing her leave.

Spatially nonsensical, Sonoma thought to herself.

Sonoma walked back into the kitchen. The lady must have run as fiercely as she presented herself, Sonoma thought, reasoning again.

"I hate this house," Sonoma said as she perused the main lobby and adjoining rooms. The rooms that were identical to her memory, a sickening corroboration of the space and the items which Sonoma had mentally inventoried. "And it hates me," Sonoma said, exiting a formal sitting room leading out to a veranda. The veranda made a loud creak as Sonoma walked on it, it screaming out in interruption like it had been awakened from a deep sleep.

Immediately, Sonoma thought of Max on the veranda at the event in Miami.

Sonoma walked through the other rooms, all similar in outdated style. Musty window treatments, beat up furniture, and dirty items filled the empty rooms.

"I want it gone," Sonoma said to the rooms and their deteriorated condition. Sonoma had made arrangements for all of the rooms' items to be removed the next day, to be extricated, taken away from the house just like she had always imagined.

Sonoma looked at her watch. The meeting was at noon, only ten minutes away. Sonoma placed the briefcase on the floor, next to her knees, they both shaking together. Sonoma then collapsed into a rickety chair by the front entrance, waiting.

Sonoma removed her cell phone from her pocket, deciding to call Max. Max knew that Sonoma would call.

Max had cleared his calendar for it, knowing that the call would happen, so that he could give Sonoma moral support.

Sonoma closed her eyes, listening nervously to the elongated rings.

Two rings…

Three rings…

Sonoma counted the rings with nervousness, wondering where Max could be.

Max answered, "My Sonoma. I thought that I'd never hear from you again," Max said with sweet charm.

Sonoma started talking rapidly, like a bullet shot out of a gun without aim or target. "Max, I'm at Café Piraza. I have the deed. I have the keys. I have it all. I know that it's happened so fast but…"

"Slow down, Sonoma," Max said sweetly, trying to ease her fast pace. "Just take a deep breath. The noon meeting will go fine."

"But what if it doesn't, Max? What am I going to do? I've got the briefcase and everything, and…"

"You will be fine, Sonoma. Trust me."

Max's voice calmed Sonoma's nerves, just like it always did when her anxiety got the best of her. Sonoma's pace slowed. "I've got so much to tell you, Max. You won't believe what happened earlier."

Sonoma told Max about the woman dressed in black on the back porch and that she supposedly lived at Café Piraza, and the details of what happened.

Max listened more than talked, which was unusual for Max. Max could hear trembling in Sonoma's voice in certain phrases, stability in others. Max sensed new patterns in Sonoma's words and the vocabulary that she chose.

Max tightened his tone, asking why Sonoma instructed

the staff to go back to the hotel.

Sonoma was perplexed at Max's knowledge.

"I know everything," Max said in a joking tone.

Sonoma didn't explain herself, and Max didn't expect her to. The mere challenge in Max's voice was all that he intended. To voice his disapproval, for Sonoma to hear, Sonoma free to take the reins after that, which is exactly what Max wanted.

Max changed the subject, talking about book events and things that had been accomplished since Sonoma had left. Sonoma missed Max deeply, and in an aching way, but Sonoma could not tell him.

At exactly twelve o'clock noon, Sonoma heard a car coming up the steep incline to Café Piraza. The meeting was now.

"I've got to go Max. They are here."

Sonoma hung up the phone without saying goodbye, her regular trademark, which Max understood more than anyone.

Gravel was flying. Dust encompassed the front entrance. The car was moving fast, like it didn't have a second to spare.

Sonoma picked up her briefcase and walked back into the kitchen. Sonoma placed it in the center of the table as the centerpiece. Twelve large chairs surrounding the gigantic, long wooden table.

The car hastily came to a stop. A split second later, the engine died.

Tears filled Sonoma eyes as she realized that her imaginings were becoming a reality.

Suddenly, a cool breeze whisked through the open kitchen window like it was announcing their arrival. Long sheer curtains bounced wildly as Sonoma peered through it. Three people were walking to the door, quickly and abrasively, like they were late but had somewhere else to be. Two women and one man with the rusty, old car sitting helplessly in the background.

Sonoma placed her hands over her mouth in fear. "I can do this," Sonoma said to herself as she walked toward the door.

A series of loud, hard knocks sounded from the foyer entrance, the door responding in hollow weakness.

Sonoma opened the door slowly, then faster with joy.

"Magda! It's you!" Sonoma screamed out in delight. "And Angeli! And Matio!" Sonoma yelled with excitement, her voice high-pitched, her eyes radiantly wide with delight and amazement.

Sonoma felt their non-reciprocal energy at the outset.

"Yes, we're here. Just as you asked," Magda responded strongly and with matter-of-factness. Magda's tone was monotone. "We're not staying long, and I'm here to do the talking. Is that understood?"

Sonoma stepped back. Disappointment began to set in. The contingent possibility of non-acceptance was unfolding before Sonoma's eyes, something that Sonoma had feared all along.

Sonoma's high energy dropped.

"Please come in," Sonoma said graciously. Sonoma lowered her head as she nimbly led them into the kitchen, trying to contain the overflowing joy that filled every ounce of her.

The three followed Sonoma mechanically, sitting down at the kitchen table without comment.

"What's that?" Magda said rudely, boisterously pointing to the briefcase in the center of the table, its body a large slab of scarred wood.

"Well," Sonoma said, "before I talk about the briefcase, I wanted to talk to you. I was hoping to learn about your life... How you are. I am so happy to see you!" Sonoma felt her energy rising, like the lid covering it could not be retrained.

The three looked at each other, offended by Sonoma's words. Magda's harsh look dominated the other two sets of eyes. All three, however, were clearly rebuffing Sonoma by their expressions.

"Look," Magda said. "Do you think you can just come in here and turn back time, like nothing ever happened? Maybe we are your brothers and sisters by blood, but we're not your family. Do you understand? We're here because you paid us to be here, and for that reason only."

Sonoma's eyes lowered in disappointment, almost shutting down in grief. For a split second, Sonoma thought of Max's counsel, his warnings of this potential, a failed meeting. Sonoma had prepared for it despite her high hopes.

Words belted from Sonoma's lips, yearning to be free, being expelled as fast as her lips could push them. "I am sorry that I left for America, leaving you here. I had no power. I had no choice. But you know that. I..."

Magda cut Sonoma off, infuriated. "Don't give me that, Sonoma. You're a liar. You left us here to perish in this maggot-filled house. And then when we finally get out, on our own, ourselves, by our fate, then you invite us back in! You even buy the godforsaken dwelling! What do you want from us? Why can't you just say it? Why are you here? What is your real motivation?" Magda's animated, livid eyes ignited the room.

Matio quietly joined in, his voice simmering with anger. "Time has driven us away, Sonoma. We are not family."

"That's right," said Angeli harshly, like a foil of Magda.

"I have children you've never seen. I struggle to buy food for my children, and you live in a mansion. Matio and I try hard to make ends meet, to live. We don't need these distractions. You're nothing but a distraction to us. That's all that you are."

Sonoma's heart sank. She could feel the crevices within her widening. Shred by shred, blow by blow, Sonoma listened to their words, tearing her apart, and feeling the vast magnitude of their anger.

Angeli exclaimed, "You don't know what our lives have been like… Where have you been through it all?"

"I know," Sonoma responded. "I know that you and Matio, being brother and sister, have children together. That you live together, that you…"

"That's not true! Matio is not my brother! I am leaving!" Angelia yelled, scooting the rustic chair back defiantly from the table, it almost turning over as she rose.

"Please don't leave," Sonoma said to Angeli desperately. "I need you here. I am here for a reason, and you are too. I want to help you."

"Help?" Magda said sarcastically in disgust.

Magda stood up with Angeli. "How could you possibly help me or any of us? You've been gone for years, decades...since you were sixteen. I was only six when you left. Matio was five, and Angeli three. Angeli doesn't even know you. Over the years, I would see your face on the cover of books in the market, in the ones that I can't read." Magda lowered her head, her voice lowering in shame as the reality of her life beset her mouth which she used as guise.

"Please… Please stay. I am here to help you, all three of you. Please hear me. I have heaviness in my heart. I am drowned by regret. I had no power to save you, to get you out of the hell…this house of monsters."

Sonoma picked up the briefcase in the center of the table. "Here's your salvation. Your new start, new beginning."

Sonoma opened the case to neatly aligned, numerous stacks of American cash bills. "It's five million dollars."

Sonoma stared into each of their eyes. The money's green color looked almost lime in the faint light. Packed neatly in tight columns and rows, the money's arrangement appeared formal and serious like the real, manifesting prosperity that the money bestowed.

"I brought this for you, my sisters and brother. Divide this money between you. I want you to start new lives. I want you to heal."

Magda laughed, "You think that paper will heal us?"

The room got silent. Sonoma felt something growing in the moment, in the soil of the air, a creation which could be a monster or a rainbow… Only time would tell.

Quiet for many seconds, Magda finally unleashed, "You think that you can just come in here and buy us? Like all those men did?"

Sonoma pursed her lips together in sorrow, shaking her head. "No, I want to help you, and me too. That's why I bought this place, this place where unforgiveable acts took place. I want everything in it destroyed. I want the monsters destroyed, to be gone forever."

The siblings desperately needed the money, but they didn't want to take it. Angeli and Matio had three young children and struggled to provide them food and clothing despite that they each worked multiple jobs. Magda had no children. Magda has lost the ability to have children at ten years old. Magda worked as a prostitute, moving each night in the darkness doing what she was taught, history repeating while Magda still dreamed of a different day.

"I'm going to leave," Magda said with hostility. "I have nothing more to say to you."

The other siblings nodded in agreement. Matio stood to join in the departure.

"Don't leave!" Sonoma yelled. Sonoma strived to regain her composure. The moment couldn't be let go. "Let me leave. Let me leave…"

Sonoma pulled the briefcase close to Magda. "Take this briefcase with you. Take it and divide it between you three. Please. For yourself, for Angeli and Matio's children. If you never see me again, take this case here today."

Sonoma left the room crying and panting, her high expectations destroyed. Sonoma ran outside. The blue sky was now black. The heavens were preparing to storm.

A cab was parked in front of Café Piraza. It was her cab driver, waiting for Sonoma, though Sonoma hadn't called him to pick her up. Somehow, he knew.

Sonoma opened the cab door and fell into the car, collapsing into the torn leather seats as Sonoma bellowed out with tears and deep groans of agony.

The cab driver didn't speak. No words. No choreographed movements. Just the free fall of the moment which was holding them both.

The cab driver started the engine. It turned over with ease. The sound of Sonoma's painful sobs commingled with the engine's spirited hum.

The cab driver saw the dots, the dots that were connected afar but with the distance removed. It was a beautiful picture, full of elaborate embellishment and detail that defied human understanding, the axel of it, however, being pain. He wished that Sonoma could see it too, the picture… And from a distance… The tapestry that was being woven, the intricate detail of the many weaving strings.

CHAPTER 22

Late that night, Sonoma went back to Café Piraza. Sonoma presumed that her siblings had left. Arriving, the cab driver cautiously drove down the path to Café Piraza with its usual style of angst.

Sonoma hoped that she would be wrong, that Magda, Angeli, and Matio would still be there, waiting for her, wanting to reunite.

Reaching the top, Sonoma's heart sank as she reconfirmed what she already knew. Magda's car was gone and so were they, lost again in the dark of the night and in the deep holes of her heart.

Sonoma got out of the car with a sense of dread and gently waved to the cab driver as he started down the drive. Sonoma would be staying the night at Café Piraza, another part of Sonoma's therapy.

Alone and in the darkness of the night, Sonoma quickly opened the front door and flipped on the lights. The foyer entranceway made a loud snapping noise at her presence. Sonoma's suitcase was by the door. The staff had brought it to Café Piraza and left it for her.

Looking at the suitcase, Sonoma shuttered at the thought of staying the night alone at Café Piraza. Sonoma felt the fear but refused to walk away.

A realization came over Sonoma. For the first time in Sonoma's life, no one was there at Café Piraza to govern her, to direct her, or mandate her actions or will.

A giant gold key then appeared in Sonoma's mind's eye. The key looked to be from the 1800's with a gold string threaded through its eye. It was the kind of key that unlocks a diary or ancient cupboard, bearing a long narrow body and single edged end. At the end of the string, was a golden tassel. It's tassel frills were thick and heavy, weighing the string down like it was too burdensome for the key to carry. For three seconds, the gold key flickered with vitality. Sonoma could see scratches glistening in the elegant detail of the key's strong, opening tooth.

Then the key disappeared, the impression dissipating into the mental matter by which it had been formed.

Immediately, Sonoma thought of a prison. Sonoma was both the prisoner and jailer. Sonoma wished for keys to unlock the jailhouse while holding the freeing keys in her hands.

Therapy, she thought again. Sonoma would stay at Café Piraza for her own wellbeing and that of Café Piraza too, the place of pirates that had stolen and shattered parts of her, the place that had encapsulated her wreckage.

Sonoma walked gingerly into the kitchen. Sonoma wanted to see if her siblings had taken the leather case.

Strewn around the room were the chairs in which her siblings had been sitting, like a rage had flown through the place and the chairs marked its path. Amidst the storm, however, the leather case was gone. Sonoma sighed in relief that her siblings had taken it, for their food and shelter, the minor exchange magnanimous to Sonoma, like the first note before a song.

"It's in motion," Sonoma said as she cleaned up the room, placing the chairs back under the table.

After unpacking her belongings and bedding, Sonoma laid down on a bed in one of the main rooms. Sonoma was exhausted from the day and the tension of the events.

Sonoma felt the softness and freshness of the clean sheets.

Sonoma lay there quiet, staring at the ceiling above her. A sky of gray, just like the building, bore zigzagged designs on its surface, imprinting in its flesh. Monsters' claw marks, Sonoma had concluded as a child.

Sonoma studied the designs more closely. A ceiling sky with no birds, no horizon, no oxygen, Sonoma thought. Only monsters... The ceiling of a child prostitution house that had operated for decades and that the government had condoned. Government men were always standing in line. It was a well-known secret in town, an oxymoron that lived, breathed, and walked by its own definition.

The phone rang.

It was Max.

Sonoma answered the phone quickly, anxious to talk to him. Max was happy to hear Sonoma's voice and she his.

The conversation was pleasant and smooth, like the feeling of touching silk after wool.

"When will it be over, Max? The torment. The rage?"

Max calculated his answer in silent pause. "When you acknowledge it. Set it free. So it can fly away to another dimension and inhabit another form."

After the phone call ended, Sonoma pondered Max's

words. "Let it go," she whispered to herself. "Inhabit another form. Leave this place."

Sonoma then drifted to sleep.

Then another flashback. That man. The coppery rattlesnake mustache. Black loomed from his eyes. His hands grabbed Sonoma's neck, choking her. "You slut! Pick up the speed!" he yelled at Sonoma. She was ten years old. The man pushed Sonoma's head into a wall. Blood splattered on it like canvas, the demons' artwork of choice. Sonoma fell to the floor. Her head was gashed, her nose broken. Blood was everywhere.

"Pick up the speed with the men here or I'll kill you!" the man screamed. "You earn your keep around here, or I'll earn you! Do you understand?" It was Ebetrio, the school master, the "line keeper."

Sonoma screamed out in terror, sitting up in the bed. Sonoma wiped the sweat from her face thinking it was blood. "It was a dream," Sonoma said to herself while crying and gasping, trying to adjust to the reality that the dream was not real. Sonoma held her face with her hands, and then hunkered down in the sheets, sobbing herself to sleep, afraid to dream.

CHAPTER 23

When Sonoma awoke the next morning, Sonoma felt energized. It was as though the terror that had drained Sonoma in her dream had somehow recharged her.

By seven a.m., Sonoma had showered and dressed. Two hours until the staff meeting, Sonoma sat in the kitchen waiting for nine o'clock to roll around.

Café Piraza was quiet, too quiet. Sonoma wished for more sound. Sonoma slowly sipped tea while reading a magazine. Each slurp sounded like an ebbing river in the quiet morning mood.

Then a knock on the door.

Sonoma stood in confusion, wondering who it could be. Sonoma went into the foyer and looked out a window. No vehicles were in sight.

Sonoma opened the door. The cool morning air greeted her with the scent of fresh rain. No one was there. Sonoma stood there a few moments.

Perplexed, Sonoma shut the door. "It must've been the wind," Sonoma said to herself as she walked back into the kitchen.

Five minutes later, Sonoma got up and checked the door again. There was no sign of anyone. Sonoma shut the door a second time.

A loud noise then came from the window, the same window that Sonoma had peered out of only moments before.

"Whoooo! Whoooo!"

A white owl was perched in the window. It was giant in size, its feathers statuesque and majestic. Small gray splotches covered its wings. Its face was brilliantly white. Its brown eyes were more vivid than any eyes that Sonoma had ever seen.

Sonoma put her hand on the glass, as if to touch it. The owl stared straight into her eyes through the pane that separated them. The white owl twitched. Sonoma twitched back.

"Whoooo! Whoooo!" the owl bellowed out again. This owl continued to stare into Sonoma's eyes.

"Hello Mr…," Sonoma said to the owl.

The owl then shook its head in a wringing fashion and flew away.

Nine o'clock rolled around. Sonoma invited the four staff members into the kitchen for their morning meeting. Sonoma greeted each of them with her usual kindness.

Sonoma went over the schedule for the day. Building crews were coming to Café Piraza to make necessary repairs, including not only the main house, but also the forty winged rooms. Demolition crews were coming to Café Piraza to take away all of the furniture and belongings. Designer crews were coming to redecorate the rooms, bringing new furniture and items to Café Piraza's, for its new beginning.

"It's going to be a long day," Sonoma said to the staff.

"I need for all of you to be here, to supervise the crews. I'll be out most of the day, so I need your help."

Sonoma's staff wasn't surprised at Sonoma's announcement of her absence. Sonoma was rarely around them despite the close connection to them she sought.

At nine thirty a.m., Sonoma's cab driver was out in front of Café Piraza waiting for Sonoma, just like Sonoma had requested. The small rusty cab was parked next to the shuttle that was still smoking from its morning trip down and up Café Piraza's drive. The cab was calm. No smoke was pouring out. It had gotten there early, to rest and regroup, knowing the tenuous journey ahead of it.

Sonoma was going to the Museum of Compilations. It was the state's government center for lodging all government registries, newspapers, and historical accounts. Sonoma's therapist had told her to go there, to learn the history of Café Piraza. It was a bullet point on Therapy plan for Sonoma's healing.

When the cab arrived at the Museum of Compilations, an hour away from Café Piraza, Sonoma was enamored with the museum's building. It was a castle. It had a drawbridge and moat that surrounded thirty acres of tightly cut pasture. Its walls were straight squares with jagged upshots, the typical castle design. Stained glass filled the windows of the castle, the style catholic medieval. The word "adventure" sounded in Sonoma's mind.

Entering the Museum of Compilations, Sonoma discovered that compilations were everywhere, records of everything that had seemingly ever happened, even records of records.

Papers, books, pamphlets, registries, newspapers… The castle was jam-packed with sortings that were intricately organized. Sonoma walked around the library's vast rooms, studying the many divisions. Sonoma found the newspaper section. The newspapers were covered in thick plastic, mummifying the newspapers' words.

After three hours of exploring and examining the newspapers, Sonoma came across a newspaper that was not in the assemblage. It was in a low shelf hidden from view an ear-shot away from the vast newspaper collection. It appeared that the newspaper had been pulled but not returned, somehow inadvertently ending up in the shelf. The newspaper was from 1949.

Sonoma admired the antiqueness of the newspaper but questioned its new-fangled appearance. The newspaper was smooth and crisp, like it had just been printed. It wasn't covered in plastic, unlike all of the other newspapers in the vast newspaper collection.

Sonoma read the newspaper in its entirety. The newspaper contained information about how Café Piraza was built in 1828 during the Argentinean civil war. Twelve provinces, who collectively called themselves the federal government, had built Café Piraza as a coffeehouse for their soldiers coming back from war. It was a place for soldiers to live and work, and Café Piraza was open to the public of the provinces to also use. The building's size was colossal for its time. The newspaper described Café Piraza as modern, describing in detail the kitchen that Sonoma had just left. The newspaper printed a picture of Café Piraza's kitchen as of 1949. In the picture, Sonoma could see an old chandelier hanging in Café Piraza's kitchen, the same one which was scheduled to be removed and replaced that very day.

Sonoma continued researching for information about Café Piraza. Sonoma explored different subject matter compilations, piecing together data that was revealed. In

1930, Café Piraza had been converted into a government school. Sonoma found old pictures of the school grounds with cotton growing in its background. In 1952, the government converted Café Piraza into an orphanage, commonly referred to a "poor house." Sonoma learned that the beginning director of it was a woman named Vivienne Stalees. Sonoma was shocked at the woman's first name.

At dusk, having spent the day at the Museum of Collections, Sonoma finally travelled back to Café Piraza. The smell of fresh pine greeted Sonoma as she walked through the front door.

Sonoma surveyed the main areas. Everything in her sight was clean, and including the kitchen whose bulky table was still angry but at the same time glad to have been bathed. The inside of Café Piraza had been thoroughly repaired, cleaned, and painted. New carpet and flooring had been installed. Modern furniture had been placed in almost every room, exactly like Sonoma had instructed. Sonoma was amazed at the results. The inside of Café Piraza looked fresh and new.

"Beautiful," Sonoma said to herself. Sonoma knew that she would sleep better that night, the fresh feel of the place already calming her.

Sonoma sat down in the kitchen to rest and have tea. Chamomile tea steamed from the teapot as she dialed Max with excitement.

Max didn't answer. Sonoma wondered where he was.

The teapot whistled. Sonoma reached for the pot, trying to avoid its steam.

Suddenly, sounding like a gunshot and hammer in unison, the teapot flew off the stove and onto the floor. The steam poured out of it, thrashing wildly, like it was having convulsions.

Sonoma screamed, jumping back, causing Sonoma to slip in the scalding water. Sonoma fell violently to the floor. The pot's boiling water scalded Sonoma's arms and hands.

The teapot then rocked back and forth, heat pulsating within it. Like it was trying to get up and do more damage, cause more carnage, cause more pain.

Sonoma shrieked and screamed as she held her burning arms and hands, small patches of skin coming off.

Sonoma ran into the bathroom and quickly turned on the water. Sonoma grabbed a towel and soaked it with cool water, wrapping her arms and hands in it like a tunnel.

Then a voice ran out. "Sonoma!"

A loud male voice yelled through the house, coming from the parlor.

Sonoma was terrified.

"Who's there!" Sonoma screamed.

There was no answer.

The house was quiet. No one was around. Several minutes passed as Sonoma stood in the bathroom, cradling her arms.

Suddenly, Sonoma felt lightheaded and dizzy. Sonoma leaned against the door. "I must be crazy," Sonoma whispered to herself as she scooted down the door with her back, still holding the cool towel around her arms like a form of protection.

Sonoma could hear the teapot. The pulsing beats in its metal body were still beating but gradually slowing, it sputtering sounding, until the beats stopped altogether.

Sonoma stood, removing the towel to look at her injured arms and hands. Second degree burns... Sonoma knew what they looked like. She'd seen them before.

Sonoma found a first aid kit underneath the kitchen sink. The crews had put it there for Sonoma, having an almost sixth sense that Sonoma would need it. Sonoma opened the first aid kit and found bandages and suave that she needed.

Sonoma dressed her wounds carefully and in silence, sitting meekly at the kitchen table. The crashed teapot was still on the floor, playing dead, mocking her. The teapot was cocked over on its side like it was watching Sonoma's demise. The teapot wanted to float…float in the ocean that it had created, water seemingly everywhere, and for Sonoma to come with it, both float away.

Inch by inch, round by round, Sonoma carefully wrapped the bandages on both arms. Deep quiet surrounded her, the richest of fertile soil where anything can happen.

Reaching the end of wrapping her arms, a brutal crash came bursting through the kitchen window behind Sonoma with speed. Glass shattered in all directions. Pieces of glass struck Sonoma in the head. Blood gushed out like a fountain.

Sonoma jumped up from the table in terror, slipping again in the water on the floor. Jagged glass sliced her legs, the blood within Sonoma finding a new doorway.

"What is going on!" Sonoma screamed out. "Who are you? What do you want?"

The newly placed designer chandelier in the kitchen started to sway. First a little, and then more, and then completely left to right with a slight and then violent, shaking bob up and down.

"What do you want from me!" Sonoma screamed, paralyzed in fear.

Then one by one, crystal droplets from the chandelier

dropped onto the table and rolled across the bulky, scarred wood. Each droplet moved like it was being pushed by an unseen force that was clearly present in the room. The droplets then rolled off the table, smashing loudly onto the floor, then rolled around in circles like they were enjoying their path.

Sonoma was speechless. Sonoma couldn't move. She was paralyzed in fear from what she was witnessing, seeing it helplessly like in a dream and without any way to stop or understand it.

Sonoma rubbed her eyes. Blood from her head was dripping into her eye lashes.

The chandelier continued to sway back and forth and bounce. The chandelier was going to fall. Sonoma knew it. The top was loose. Wires were protruding from its encasement ready to spring free.

Sonoma struggled to escape. Badly cut and injured and paralyzed in fear, Sonoma crawled through the kitchen to the foyer door dragging a piece of glass embedded in her leg.

The front door slammed open with fierce indignity, making a dent in the wall. The door rapidly came to a halt.

The foyer window then scrolled up with venomous energy, glass shattering all around Sonoma, more glass making its way into her.

Sonoma screamed out in panic, trying to crawl toward the parlor. The parlor was now modern red and was bright and energetic, not the cool coral that Sonoma had seen when she got home.

Sonoma lay in the parlor floor. Blood dripped from her head and face onto the new marble floor.

And there, in front of her, a nightmare manifested. It was the idol of fear, Ebetrio.

Ebetrio was standing over her with a depraved look on his face. He was carrying the old rusty axe and a piece of umbilical cord dangling from its blade. Ebetrio looked the same as Sonoma remembered and which her memories portrayed. His mustache was curved sinfully outward from his face, like he had two extra fingers on his head, pointing to everyone but himself.

Ebetrio's face was red. His eyes were black. Ebetrio's suspenders held up his carefully pressed pants so that they wouldn't fall down, at least not until he wanted them to fall, like a tree.

Sonoma had seen Ebetrio in her flashbacks, but never in this quality of vision.

Ebetrio glared at Sonoma.

Sonoma struggled to find courage. Sonoma knew that Ebetrio was not of this world.

Ebetrio opened his mouth, his gums visibly black as he spoke from a backlit glow all around him. "You made it back," Ebetrio said slowly and with a growl. "I told you that I'd kill you if you ever left me." Ebetrio laughed hysterically, his mustache bouncing up and down in hysteria like the unbalanced bobbling of the kitchen chandelier.

Sonoma covered her eyes with her bandaged arms, shaking, just like she did as a child.

The word "courage" came into Sonoma mind.

"What do you want?" Sonoma to Ebetrio slowly and precisely, still covering her eyes with her bandaged arms.

Seconds went by with no response. Sonoma put her arms down to her side, air warming around her.

The apparition was gone.

Sonoma struggled to get her phone out of her pocket. It finally fell to the floor. Sonoma repeatedly tried to dial for emergency help with her bandaged arms.

Sonoma then heard a little boy cry out. "Help me!"

Sonoma heard other voices of children too, young girls and boys. Each and all cried out to help them, to take them away. "I don't want to be here!" a girl screamed. "Leave me alone!" another girl said to a man. Sonoma then heard sounds of gunshots. Sounds of rape. Sounds that as they emerged, Sonoma newly recalled them. The sounds had been blocked from Sonoma's memory, tracing back in her life as young as three months old.

Sonoma crawled back into the kitchen. The chandelier was hunched over on the table like a mushroom. Many of its limbs had broken off and were on the floor. Some were bent like antennas and fine sculptures, looking for any signals of life. The chandelier had fallen, just like her.

As Sonoma lay there on the watered floor waiting for help, the moonlight beamed through Café Piraza's broken window with passion, enjoying its close connection to her. The present moment comforted Sonoma, despite the terrorizing contents. It was like time stood still and created a new type of time, inconsistent with time as we know it, inconsistent with fear. Filled with only love holding fear in its hands. Sonoma was stilled, like a mother bird was standing over her, its baby bird, preparing to teach her to fly.

CHAPTER 24

Sonoma awoke in the hospital.

Soft afternoon light veered in through the window warming Sonoma's bandaged hands that lay to her side. Sonoma flickered her eyes slightly open, trying to adjust to the light.

Sonoma found herself alone in the quiet room. Sonoma recollected the prior night's events. The sights, the sounds, the realness of what happened.

A voice gently sounded. "I'm here."

Sonoma turned her head. It was Max. Max had been watching Sonoma sleep. Max had been watching Sonoma fight memories, imprints of the past. Max had gotten there two hours ago, immediately boarding a plane once he got word of the accident.

"My Max," Sonoma whispered gently. "You are here," Sonoma said smiling.

Max walked over to Sonoma and touched her lips gently with his finger. "I am here, and I will always be here. You need to rest right now. I talked to the doctors."

A nurse came in and gave Sonoma medication to calm her.

"I'm going back there you know," Sonoma said to Max as she drifted.

"I know that you are," Max said, patting Sonoma's shoulder. "You need to sleep."

For three days, Max stayed at Sonoma's side in the hospital, caring for her. Lacerations, bruises, and burns were Sonoma's injuries. Sonoma would recover fully with time.

Three days later, leaving the hospital, Sonoma demanded that Max take her back to Café Piraza.

"Has anyone been to Café Piraza since my accident?"

"Just me. I sent the staff back to Miami. I figured that since I was here, they could work back home. I also told work crews to hold off for a few days."

As they arrived at Café Piraza, travelling down the steep hill and then up the incline, Sonoma was overcome with fear. Sonoma thanked God that Max was with her.

The car came to a stop. Sonoma opened the car door puzzled.

"How can it be?" Sonoma said slowly, trying to understand the scene before her. The foyer window was intact, not broken at all. "Did you replace the window, Max?"

"No."

Max shut the car door behind him. Max walked around to Sonoma. "No one did."

Thirty seconds went by.

"The window's not broken," Sonoma said in disbelief. Sonoma faced the window in confusion.

Max watched Sonoma absorb the reality.

"Let's talk about it later, what you say happened."

Sonoma opened the door to Café Piraza and walked

inside. It was clean and pristine, just like the decorators had left it.

Sonoma walked to the kitchen, covering her mouth when she got inside.

The chandelier was hanging above the table in perfect condition. Its multitudes of crystal droplets were glistening in the sun against the ornate cast bronze that dangled the crystals with pride.

Sonoma studied the chandelier and the floor.

Sonoma studied the teapot on the counter.

All were unharmed and in perfect order like there had never been a disturbance. Just like it had been when Sonoma returned from the Museum of Collections, as if the scene were playing over again.

Max dove into the conversation in Sonoma's mind. "I think that you were dreaming."

"No," Sonoma said adamantly. "I was not dreaming. I was not asleep. It was real."

At the hospital, Sonoma had told Max everything that had happened, and including the frightful apparition, voices, and sounds and the rage that she saw in Ebetrio's eyes.

"This house is alive," Sonoma said.

"You should stay somewhere else. I've got reservations at The Inn."

"No. I'm not leaving. I've got to stay here," Sonoma declared.

"I can't leave you alone, Sonoma."

"You can. Alone is all that I ever knew in this place."

"Well, then I'll stay with you, if that's okay."

"Of course," Sonoma said nonchalantly, sitting down at the kitchen table and staring up at the chandelier, then slowly breaking free from her stare. It was okay, more than okay. Sonoma yearned for Max to stay with her.

Max purposefully changed the subject. "I've heard so much about this place through the years."

Sonoma shook her head, now fully snapped out of her daze. "I'll show you around."

For years, Sonoma had told Max about Café Piraza. Sonoma had described it in so many different settings and ways. In private dinners, in meetings, in therapy, when they were alone, Sonoma told Max about things that had happened while growing up at Café Piraza, but far from everything. There were things that Sonoma couldn't talk about with anyone, even Max. There were things that Sonoma couldn't remember but felt the evil memories' presence as she went about her life each day. There were some good memories too, most of them made in the library or outside bench where Sonoma often escaped to learn or play. And of course the pasture, which was Sonoma's sanctuary.

Through numerous rooms of Café Piraza, on both wings, Sonoma walked Max through Café Piraza, now resembling a high-end hotel. The work crews had done excellent repair and restoration work, as well as redecoration. Each room had a new, updated look and décor, which was pleasant to Sonoma's eye. Despite the new appearance of the rooms, however, Sonoma could still sense a presence that hadn't changed. It was like rooms were silently communicating with Sonoma, her memory acknowledging them, telling Sonoma that they would not change, no matter the frills or paint.

A warm afternoon breeze came through as Max and Sonoma turned back to go to the main building. The tour was complete.

"Café Piraza has charm," Max said, walking down the connecting corridor.

"So does the devil," Sonoma responded.

Max grabbed Sonoma's hand.

Sonoma smiled, child-like and enamored. Max had never grabbed Sonoma's hand before in that certain intimate way.

Max's handsome blue eyes warmed his dark black hair. Max's fit and muscular frame appeared more relaxed than Sonoma remembered, less formal than his usual stance. The pause between them was palpable.

"When I got the call…that you were in the hospital…," Max began.

Max stopped and looked into Sonoma's eyes.

"…it was like my heart stopped. I came here as fast as I could. I could never live without you, and I've never told you."

So many times Max had wanted to kiss Sonoma. So many times Max had wanted to feel Sonoma's blonde hair, spun gold, so exotic, so rare. To touch Sonoma, caress her, become one with her. All against his better judgment, his business plans, and his safeguards, rules that Max had never broken before.

And in that moment, Max gave in. Max kissed Sonoma. Long and passionate, it was a kiss that cannot be replicated. Time stood still for both of them, the present being all that mattered.

Max held Sonoma tightly in his arms as he embraced her passionately for the first time, just as he had always imagined and yearned to do.

Sonoma wanted Max too. Sonoma melted in Max's arms, acquiescing in the embroil burning within him.

Max knew it and seized Sonoma, frantically undressing her with his hands, his body, his breath overshadowing her. Blissfully complacent, Sonoma then seized Max back, taking him as much as he was taking her. Instinctually, Max laid Sonoma down on the rock pathway, the beauty of her nakedness overpowering him. Max saw it. Max felt it, the true beauty of love. He was a part of Sonoma, a control which he held onto tightly, more controlling than lust could ever be.

Max kissed Sonoma's breasts, overflowing with life. Max quickly unbuttoned his shirt, revealing his muscular tone. Sonoma removed Max's shirt, throwing it to the side. Sonoma's lips and nipples overtook Max, filling him with ecstasy. Max then entered Sonoma, consummating what had always existed between them. The warmth, the connection, their urges surpassing, Max and Sonoma climaxed together, repeatedly, in the warm, afternoon air at the most unlikely place that had brought them together, a bridge born of rawness and pain. And as the day matured, so did Café Piraza, its dwelling quiet and composed, no distractions in sight.

CHAPTER 25

Max sat up and looked at the clock. It was 3:00 a.m.

Sonoma was sleeping soundly next to him.

Max climbed gingerly out of the bed and walked out of the room.

Max shut the door then covered his eyes with his hands. "What have I done?"

Max grabbed a t-shirt and boxers out of his suitcase, putting them on in the kitchen.

Max then got a glass of water. The house was quiet. Max drank the water slowly and deliberately, his usual way of consumption.

Max leaned over the kitchen sink with his glass. Max knew that he had crossed the line.

Finishing the water, Max put the glass in the sink.

Then three loud, agitated knocks sounded from the front foyer door.

Max let out an angry moan running quietly to the door.

Max opened the door. It was Magda.

"I told you to be quiet. And here you knock?" Max scolded.

Max pushed Magda to the side, out of his way, and walked onto the porch, shutting the door quietly behind him.

Magda was dressed in a provocative black dress which hugged her body from every angle. Her shiny long brown hair hung past her shoulders. Magda was smoking a cigarette, the burn of it as red as her lipstick, which Magda inhaled deeply and strongly. Magda's dark eyes contrasted with her pale skin, emphasizing a three inch scar visibly on her forehead.

For a split second, Magda resembled Sonoma. Max shook it off.

Magda's rusty green car was running. Max could see Matio and Angeli in the backseat. Both were wearing hats. Cigarette smoke poured out of their mouths and from their partially cracked windows.

"I presume that you got the money," Max said to Magda.

"I did. I got it. Five million," Magda answered coldly. Magda then bellowed out loudly laughing with a half-smiled smirk, "Sonoma is so stupid. We're leaving this dump, this god awful place. You got that!"

"Be quiet," Max scolded her. "You'll wake Sonoma."

"Whatever, you fool! You're crazy to love Sonoma. She's a whore just like me!"

Magda's loudness was purposeful. Max sensed Magda's intent to wake Sonoma up.

Max dragged Magda off the porch with her arm, her cigarette still flaming like red burning coal. Max yelled in a muffled voice, his voice a stifled canon positioned to strike. "You're going to wake her! And you want to! I can see it in your eyes!"

Magda took another puff from her cigarette combined with a wicked, repelling laugh.

"You got the money, Magda. Confirmation is complete. So leave! Leave us alone!"

"Us?" Magda said with emphasis, continuing her staving laugh. "Leave us alone? Are you kidding me?" Magda harshly thundered out laughing. Cigarette smoke followed her shaking head.

"Leave!" Max said to Magda. "Don't ever come back. You got the money just like you demanded. Now leave Sonoma alone. Don't think about her, not even once. Your thoughts are poison."

"And how will you know if I think about her, Max? Or if I think about you? I have a lot to think about, you know. All those nights with you at The Inn all those years ago while you studied Sonoma."

"You extorted me," Max said.

"You fucked me."

Magda threw her cigarette on the stone pathway. "You're pathetic. You're not even real."

Like a nerve had been hit, Magda then struck Max in the face. "Did you feel that?"

Magda barraged Max, like a spider challenging an elephant, inviting Max to fight physically. "Come on!"

Max struggled to contain himself. Max touched his cheek. Warm blood streamed from his nose. Max wanted to kill Magda.

Realization of what Magda had done dawned upon her.

Magda ran to her car and flung open the door hysterically, like she was mentally deranged and reality had just opened its dark bag.

Magda slammed the car door with a loud clash, like the sound a magician makes when he pulls a tablecloth from underneath pans and one flies off, whanging the ground.

Magda threw the car's gear in drive and hit the accelerator. Magda fired off, stripping gears back and forth, as she darted down the steep hill like a blackbird in swoop.

Max went over and sat down on the bench.

Max removed his t-shirt to soak up the blood. His nose, though not broken, had been badly assaulted.

Max thought that he deserved it.

CHAPTER 26

By morning, Max had cleaned himself up and disposed of his bloody shirt. The night's events had been concealed, hiding them in the darkness from whence they came.

The new day began radiantly. The mood of the morning felt like the energy of a tulip opening its arms to a sunshine-filled sky. Slowly yawning with the sun, then opening blissfully with ease.

Awakening with happiness, Sonoma lifted her head to see Max sitting next to her, fully dressed and holding a mug of hot coffee. A cup of freshly brewed jasmine tea sat on the nearby table for Sonoma, Sonoma's favorite.

"What time is it?" Sonoma asked.

"Noon," Max said between a sip while reading the news on his phone. "I let you sleep."

"Noon?" Sonoma said, rising frantically. "I haven't slept to noon in years."

Sonoma plopped back down on the pillow, consciously discarding her unorthodox, late slumber.

"Noon...," Sonoma said to herself again with a laugh.

The day was gloriously beautiful. The sun was shining in the pleasant temperature of seventy-five.

"I have plans for us today," Max said to Sonoma smiling, his eyes still glued to his phone, reading.

"Of course," Sonoma said smiling, feeling the soft pillow on her face.

The drive took an hour.

Max took back roads, rarely used roads that surrounded Café Piraza which locals ignored, other roads now paved, smoother ways.

The roads' twisting, winding turns gave Café Piraza's driveway an appreciable reprieve. The roads were equally, if not more, disturbed than the private drive of Café Piraza, having a marked, confused make and condition of its own land which seemed to never end.

Almost no other cars were on the road. Despite the land's curved, jarring physique, the scenes of the peaceful countryside were magnificent. They passed a giant river with a commanding, thrashing waterfall, an amazing sight. Birds were drinking the water from the top of the fall, like God had made the abundant, flowing stream just for them, no fear of falling in their eyes.

A line of turtles crossed the road like Russian matryoshka nesting dolls. The father and mother turtles led the line of birthed children across the road with confidence that they would all see the light of the next day. Max stopped the car to watch, the spectacular scene both a bookmark and parable of the story of their lives.

Max and Sonoma enjoyed their conversation during the drive. They enjoyed seeing the varying landmarks and views of Argentina, many of which Sonoma had never seen despite her years of living in the region.

Max then reached the large, ornate hotel called "The Inn."

Sonoma's heart melted. "It's the same one that we stayed at before... When I was reunited with Aubella."

"I wanted to bring you back here. For you... For Aubella.. . For us," Max said with a nervous smile. "For us," Max said slowly repeating.

"I'd like to spend the day here, if that's okay."

Max pulled around the circular front of the hotel as an entourage approached to valet the car.

Max got out of the car nervously. Max grabbed Sonoma's hand and led her into the hotel. Max could barely breath.

Immediately, Max led Sonoma onto an elevator.

The elevator attendant looked at Max.

"The tenth floor," Max ordered, though entwined with resistance.

The tenth floor button lit up, the button that was a never-ending candle lighting pathways for others but stuck in its own stagnant glow.

The elevator doors closed. They then arrived.

When the doors opened, Sonoma was surprised to find that the tenth floor was the top of The Inn. The tenth floor had no ceiling. It's only further height was the blue sky and the winds that engulfed it. Tables upon tables were laid out in columns on the floor, a massive area for visiting and dining, for people to enjoy the divinely fresh, unbridled air. An intricate railing encircled the space like a gentle hand protecting its contents.

Max took Sonoma to the small, private table that he had reserved.

The view was spellbinding.

A sea of mountains filled the distance. Serenity

exuded their collective stance.

An infinity-size bouquet of flowers filled the up-close view along with gossamer greenery that connected to the flowers' stems. Flowers mingled...stood...sat...all at the same time and in different ways, and in every conceivable style and color.

A stream flowed between the two views, merging them together. Sonoma felt like she was sitting with nature, mother earth herself. The words "On Defining God" sounded in Sonoma's mind. Just like Sonoma had heard before, from the source within her who had named Sonoma's garden.

"Words cannot express the beauty...," Sonoma said while being seated. "It's like entering God's garden in the sky that matches ours below, if only we'd see."

Max felt the import of Sonoma's words.

"It is," Max said in response.

The two ate lunch, enjoying each other as much as the views.

Max searched for the right moment to bring up the inevitable.

After many foregone opportunities, like the beauty of the garden, Max struggled for words to express.

Himself...what Max was feeling inside, what Max needed to say.

Max pushed ill-chosen words out of him. "I need to talk with you, Sonoma...about something different."

Max's words came out awkwardly and forcibly, but out nonetheless.

"Sure," said Sonoma. "Do you want to discuss upcoming book details or..."

"No," Max interrupted. "Not that."

Max stammered. Max's words fell out awkwardly again. "It's hard to articulate. I figured that coming here, seeing the skyline, would help me initiate the discussion."

Sonoma was intrigued but not surprised. Max's style had always been complex. Sonoma listened with patience.

"I want to talk about what happened to you. At Café Piraza, when I wasn't there."

"Yes," Sonoma said slowly with interest.

Max took a deep breath.

"I know what happened to you."

Max was serious, as serious as Sonoma had ever seen him.

"You saw residual energy. That's what you experienced in the house."

Sonoma shook her head, not understanding.

"Residual energy…," Max said again. "That's what you saw. You saw energy of traumatic events or intense emotion."

"I don't understand."

"Let me explain it this way to you… When the earthly spirit, the energetic body, fractures, splinters, or shatters from trauma, it is damaged. Though 'damaged' isn't the right word…"

Max continued to struggle for words. "The word 'changed' is more accurate. The spirit is changed, and the change can manifest in various degrees and ways. Trauma that causes a chip can turn into a splinter, which can turn into a fracture, which can turn into a shattering. In any change, however, despite the manner, *energy dissociates* from the spirit, and in varying degrees. Trauma freezes thinking, although trauma has an intelligence of its own."

Max paused but then continued. "The change takes on a new life, a new incarnation, with corresponding repercussions. There is great truth when someone who has been traumatized says that 'a part of them died.' Or, 'that they moved on' or 'were reborn.'"

Sonoma continued listening.

"Often, the spiritual change, we'll call it a 'spiritual fracture' - the energetic vibration of it, wave - attaches to the material world. The material world strives to retain its possession in fear of losing it. At the same time, the spiritual fracture fights to escape being possessed. A war between them develops, causing a merged residual loop to be formed. The loop has no beginning or end. The loop of traumatic events plays over and over as traumatic memory, though not always in the same form. But in similar form, by fractal design. It's no different than our own memory, when we replay events in our mind and the storytelling slightly varies."

Sonoma appraised Max's words.

Sonoma reached for a glass of water, trying to likewise wash the information down. "It sounds complicated."

"Residual energy is as complex as an individual's personality. Like shades of colors, like times of day, residual energy expresses itself in varying degrees and binds in different ways. It usually appears as an energy loop that plays over and over, 'non-intelligent' as people like to call it, which is a misnomer as I said before, though not 'intelligent' in the way commonly understood. There are also residuals within residuals, a form of hybrid life within merged worlds."

"How do we stop the loops?" Sonoma asked.

"Many spirits, people who have died, don't want the loops stopped because they are attracted to the residual energy. These are spirits who still want to be in the physical world for whatever reason. The loops are like doors half open to them, giving them glimpses onto the other side."

Max felt bewilderment in Sonoma's voice.

"So, what you're saying is…that I saw energy embedded in Café Piraza," Sonoma said, picking up her glass of water again.

"Yes, but you also saw energy embedded in you that has changed."

"It just seems so impossible," Sonoma said, pushing her glass of water to the side.

"How is it impossible? Café Piraza is a treasure trove of pain."

Max pointed to the mountains. "See the mountains?"

Sonoma looked at the panoramic view of the majestic mountains in the distance.

"Do you see the peaks of them?" Max said, purposefully pausing again.

"Yes."

"The peaks are points of energy, no different than a pyramid, morphed by the land's growth. Going down the mountain are sediments, layers of residual energy, no different than Café Piraza or any other place, even you. All are spiritual landscapes.

"That makes sense."

"Think of all the millions of years that have passed since the mountains were made. Men have died climbing the mountains.   Erosions and storms have morphed them. Think about the energetic markings left on the mountains themselves, its land bursting from its seams to go in another direction, making change."

"What about happiness?" Sonoma asked. "Doesn't happiness count? Are there happiness-filled residuals?"

Max smiled, "The intense emotion, happiness, sediments too. Happiness is a shade of love, and love is the essence of expression."

Sonoma pondered Max's teaching further.

"I want to make the traumatic energy go away. I want it to leave me alone."

"You can. But you must reclaim your power from the looped energy. Call the energy back. Bring it back. Undo the spell that's causing the circular loop. You do this by controlling the trauma - in the present moment - by allowing the energy to express itself. When you do this, immediately, the war stops. The energy loses all interest and obsession in the fight. The material world doesn't want the fracture because it has expressed and defined itself and can't be possessed. The spiritual fracture has expressed and defined itself so it has no fear of being possessed and can't be possessed. The energy becomes attachment-free and expression-complete. As result, the spiritual fracture moves on, resulting in a cataclysm borne by its own fracture, inhabiting a different form or even formless form."

"You actually believe that intention, calling back one's power, can change a supernatural energy?"

Max laughed. "Intention is supernatural energy. There's no coincidence that the word 'tent' is in the word 'intention.' The tent, the peak, is the essence of pyramidal energy, the ultimate way to funnel source. Man is supernatural. Spirit is natural."

Sonoma questioned Max the rest of the afternoon.

Slowly, the mood tilted in a new direction, Sonoma's eyes wide open all the while. The universe's axel was in process, a cataclysm emerging of its own.

CHAPTER 27

Max and Sonoma didn't arrive back to Café Piraza until eight p.m.

The day had been long. Both were exhausted from the long afternoon and complex discussions.

"It's simply complicated," Sonoma said laughing as Max opened the door to Café Piraza.

"That's what we should name the next yacht that the foundation buys, 'Simply Complicated,'" Max said back in jest, then taking off his tie, ready to unwind.

Max kissed Sonoma gently on her lips to preface a statement, but which suddenly fell away.

Then out of nowhere, like Max's spirit of chipped stones was doused with radiant light, the statement found him. Words that Max had coveted and hungered for Sonoma to say, and he hear...

Sonoma whispered, "I have always loved you, Max."

The remainder of the evening was quiet.

It was like Sonoma's words that had taken Max by storm had fallen but at the same time risen to a new level and were adjusting to the height.

Sonoma took a hot bath, relaxing in the heat of the water and quietness all around her.

Max was handling business on his computer in the kitchen.

Sonoma then got into bed to settle down for the night, only a room away from Max in proximity. Lying in bed, Sonoma could see Max through a connecting doorway to the kitchen. Max's profile was handsome and sleek. Sonoma watched Max move every few minutes while typing on his computer. Max's movements were predictable. Max moved in patterns, even down to subtle twitches of his eyes. Max's cheek would dimple when he would start a new paragraph, a pattern which Sonoma noticed after many minutes of astute study.

Sonoma thought about the day and the information that Max had given her. Sonoma pondered it professionally, with her background and training. Sonoma pondered it personally, knowing that Max was always right. Sonoma thought about the foyer and kitchen windows that had shattered, now uninjured. How else could it be explained? How could the windows now be unbroken and the chandelier intact?

Sonoma looked at her arms. The bandages were real.

Sonoma fell asleep.

Almost an hour later, at precisely eleven p.m., a loud crash sounded in the kitchen.

Sonoma jumped out of bed and ran through the connecting doorway.

"Max!" Sonoma screamed.

The chandelier had fallen, just like it had before. Crystals were frenziedly rolling across the table and bouncing onto the tile floor and travelling in circles.

Max was sitting at the table in his same working position, buried beneath the debris.

Max's blood was everywhere.

Max's computer was in countless pieces on the floor.

Then the sounds again, that Sonoma had heard the days prior. A young girl cried out, "Help me!" screaming loudly.

And then the others. Voices of children, young girls and boys crying out. "I don't want to be here!" a girl screamed. "Leave me alone!" a girl said to a man. Sounds of gunshots. Sounds of rape. Just like Sonoma had heard before though with hints of variation.

Sonoma struggled to remove the chandelier from the table. Its colossal, mushroom frame was tangled and twisted. The chaos covered Max's face.

"Please be alive!" Sonoma screamed. "Max! Max!"

Max's eyes were slightly open. Max didn't realize what had happened.

Max had a severe head wound. A two inch gash was cut deeply into his head.

Sonoma frantically reached for her phone on the counter, to call for emergency help.

"Don't call them," Max said, groaning.

Sonoma had already stated dialing.

"I'll be okay," Max said with increasing alertness. "Just call it back. Now!"

Sonoma felt helpless and weak, skewed in so many ways, like she was a piece of paper being torn.

The voices continued.

The loops.

The children.

A young girl then appeared, like a black and white silhouette, visible in front of Sonoma.

Sonoma dropped her phone, it crashing onto the floor. The crystal droplets were still moving across the table, the same invisible hand pushing them over and for their plunge to the floor.

Sonoma unruffled herself, trying to calm the layers within her. "Be brave," Sonoma thought.

The young girl softly whispered to Sonoma, "I am with you."

Sonoma shook her head. Sonoma then remembered. The girl was her. It was Sonoma as a young girl. So pretty, so sweet, but ravaged by poverty, sexual abuse, and rage.

"I am with you," the young girl said to Sonoma again, as the torturous sounds continued.

Then he appeared again, Ebetrio. His wiry mustache was no longer copper, but rusty, putrid green. "So am I!" Ebetrio yelled to Sonoma with a revolting grin, casting and inflicting his black, glowing eyes upon Sonoma.

The room then instantly re-set, like time had reversed.

The chandelier was hanging perfectly intact from the kitchen ceiling.

Max's computer was on the table, its pieces reconnected, back together.

Max was sitting there, unharmed, the order having returned.

Shaken, confused, and silent, Sonoma started gasping for air. Sonoma felt like she was drowning in the room.

"It's okay," Max said. "You are adjusting dimensionally. You are growing lungs, dimensional lungs."

Max held Sonoma tightly until her gasping subsided. Max caressed her long blonde hair with his hands as Sonoma wept, pushing her hair to one side. Max then kissed Sonoma's scar which was now visible, the vicious

brand from her past.   Now brimming with beginning,
channeling their connection to a higher realm that they
would forever share.

CHAPTER 28

"I'm leaving," Sonoma said to Max firmly while packing her clothes.

Max roused from his thin veil of sleep.

"What?" Max jumped up. "Why? Why are you leaving?"

It was four a.m.

"Why do you think? This place is haunted, and so am I. I have got to leave. I have got to leave everywhere, if that can be done."

"You shouldn't leave."

"You didn't even want me to come here, Max. I should've listened to you."

Sonoma slammed her suitcase shut on the bed and closed the closet doors.

Max strong-holded Sonoma's body. "You're not going anywhere," Max said firmly, holding her body in place with his strong body and arms.

"Don't you see?" Sonoma bellowed out. "I'm affected by this place, affected by the torment, the memories, my memories, the abuse. It will never go away."

Max dropped his arms.

Sonoma sat on the bed, sobbing. "I don't care anymore. I'm leaving this place. I've tried to face it."

Max sat down on the bed with Sonoma.

"I can't face it for you, Sonoma," Max said, kissing her hands. "But we can face it together, you and me. The way it has been planned…"

Sonoma heard the sounds of Max's words, but the significance of them slipped by her. Sonoma tightly hugged Max's body, falling into his muscles, strengthening her. Max then stretched Sonoma out on the bed, making love to her in the early morning. Quiet this time, the tension slowly releasing from their bodies as they united, merging under the cool white sheet that was a penumbra of their forever union.

"I knew you wouldn't leave," Max whispered to Sonoma, then powerfully climaxing within her. As Max's body protracted, Sonoma felt his pulsation within her. Sonoma instinctively let go, culminating with obsession, spellbound once again.

CHAPTER 29

The early morning elevated energy lingered until nine a.m. when Max rose from the bed to take a shower.

Sonoma was sleeping peacefully.

The showering water fell on Max's face like masculinity defined. Max bathed his sculpted muscular frame as manly as he appeared. The water beat down upon his skin with a soft whooshing sound. Max embraced the pounding water and its therapeutic, freeing force.

Max then heard Sonoma's voice in the background. She had risen for the day. Sonoma's sweet voice was pleasantly muffled by the sound of the moving water and Max's movements within it.

A thump. Something opened. Max heard Sonoma move about. Max loved the sounds, Sonoma's stirrings. She was taking care of him, nurturous acts, cooking him breakfast, Max knew. Max was enthralled at the intimate connections with Sonoma that had long been omitted from his life.

Then the sound of gunfire went off in the shower, right next to Max's head. Max jumped back with alarm, shocked and dumbfounded at the explosive sound.

Max could hear his own voice moaning, "I am dying."

Max instinctively held his chest. Pain was emanating from it.

Max then saw tangible images before him, remembrances of his life. It was 1828, the year visible on a town clock which appeared. Max was a soldier. Max had been shot in battle and was on the ground dying as a coverture of gun smoke formed circular rings above him.

Max then saw images from a different perspective. Max was in the sky, looking down. Soldiers were dying next to him. Gun smoke covered the setting like a dense, but see-through veil.

Max felt his consciousness moving into another dimension.

Effortlessly…

Max's vision was blurring.

Max's eyes then saw nothing but black, like the light went off and the water too.

And then the lights… The lights came upon him, giving new, multi-faceted meaning to the word glory. Billions of brilliant diamond lights were all around Max, flashing white and shimmering rainbows of color. The lights had seen Max in the darkness. They had rushed to his side.

Max touched one, feeling the band of its breadth. Individual, yet collective, a piece of salt of the earth.

"Design with the fractures," the light said wordlessly to Max.

The lights then lined up in unison, forming a perfectly straight line. The lights were soldiers lining up, holding hands instead of guns, having found a better way than winning or losing.

The ends of the line then began rounding...curving...until each end of the line met, forming a perfect circle the size of all of the universe's suns and moons put together.

Max disembarked again.

Max jolted away, and then fell.

Falling back into the shower, the hot water pouring like liquid gold onto his body, nature's mold.

Max quickly shut off the shower.

The water ceased abruptly as Max stood there naked, his chest now alleviated but his breath heavy and strained.

Sonoma yelled to Max from a distance. "I made breakfast for you. I've got some business to do. I'll be back."

Max heard Sonoma's words.

Clicks and clangs were then audible, and then hasty movements in the foyer and then outside.

Max scrambled and shuttered. Max didn't want Sonoma to leave or be alone. Max leapt out of the shower and ran to the bedroom window. The window's sheer panels rustled with his movement, attaching to Max's wet body as he stood there naked staring out.

It was the cab driver, picking up Sonoma to transport her. Max knew him. Max also knew the planned destination.

CHAPTER 30

"I'll be here till three," Sonoma said to the cab driver as she exited.

The driver acknowledged Sonoma's agenda with plans to pick her up later that day.

An elderly gentleman approached Sonoma. "Welcome to The Inn."

The man's words sounded mechanical to Sonoma, like an oiled hinge in motion, in process. Sonoma recognized his face from the day prior.

The man opened the large gold doors leading into the hotel lobby.

Sonoma walked in, almost fainting.

Sonoma was stunned. Everything was different. The décor, the furniture, and the pictures on the wall had completely changed from the day prior, and including the texture of the walls and floors. The soothing, calming expression of The Inn had disappeared. Its energy was high voltage.

The floor was no longer tranquil marble with black and gray veins, but shiny black, brandishing every imprint and smudge with the highest of discrimination.

The walls were no longer comfortingly texturized and camouflaged, but sleek and smooth where any error in the wall would be immediately exposed. Bright red and orange colors saturated the walls, like a two-toned painter's palette had fallen from the sky to increase the vibration. Matching red and orange flowers filled the lobby in various breeds, some solid in color, others splotched with design. The blooms' texture was unnatural, appearing like leather.

Sonoma studied the flowers, the science that she knew. "There's no way that these breeds come in these colors or texture," Sonoma to herself, while walking around the room like an explorer, examining them. It was like The Inn had grown new senses overnight and was expressing them in Sonoma's presence, a concept foreign to Sonoma and which Sonoma knew was astray.

Sonoma sensed another mechanical rhythm in process. "Will you be staying with us?" said a lady dressed in white, politely, her pleasantry rote.

"I will. But I want the largest suite that you have, no matter the cost."

Sonoma looked away from the lady dressed in white. Sonoma's eyes were glued to the elevator. "I'll first be dining on the tenth floor. With the skyline, the mountain view."

Sonoma then turned back around, again facing the lady in white.

"Wonderful," the lady said, her roteness wrapping up.

The lady then disappeared for a few minutes. Sonoma continued to walk around the lobby, studying the flowers and the intricate designs of their blooms. The flowers hadn't been there yesterday when she had been there with Max.

"Here are your keys. You're all set." The lady in white handed Sonoma the keys, multiple keys to all of the rooms in the largest suite. The keys were gold with etched markings, the same ones that Sonoma had seen in her mind after days before.

Sonoma got on the elevator. The elevator was different too. Its walls were gold, etched with scratches, just like the keys in her hand.

Arriving at the tenth floor, the elevator door opened.

"This can't be," Sonoma said exiting. "This isn't the same place." Sonoma could not believe what she was seeing.

"May I help you get seated?" a young waiter said to Sonoma. "Is this your first time dining here?"

The young waiter sounded mechanical too, premeditated and rehearsed. And for the first time, Sonoma heard ticks and tocks of mechanical rhythm all around her. The people, the sights, the sounds, the process, and the everything around her were operating with measured sounds, measured waves, measured beats, like the running heartbeat of a giant clock.

Sonoma was silent in response to the waiter's question. But it didn't matter. The waiter took Sonoma to the very same table that she and Max had dined at the day prior.

Sonoma sat down in the same chair.

The condiments were lined up the same way as the day before.

Another waiter came over and poured water for Sonoma, only a hint of variance from the day before.

No other customers were dining, just like the day before.

Sonoma sat there in disbelief, gazing out over the wrought iron railing. A turquoise blue ocean surrounded her. No mountains were in sight. Seagulls chirped and squawked playfully, enjoying the day. The weather was slightly warmer than the day before. The sun felt good on Sonoma's pale, delicate cheeks, absorbing the heat as it radiated down upon her and the sights before her eyes.

Sonoma was calm, though shocked at the sight. Sonoma sat muted for an hour, watching and listening. Looking at the skyline, the horizon, the place where she had seen mountains that were now gone. "Did the tide sweep the mountains away?" Sonoma said to herself, half-laughing in private.

Sonoma then left the table to go to her suite. Sonoma had seen enough of the tenth floor.

Opening its large doors, the suite was palatial and refined. The suite was decorated with lime green and soft colors. Sonoma noticed the entranceway chandelier. It was an exact replica of the new chandelier in Café Piraza's kitchen, the one that had fallen, over and over, but somehow regenerated itself and reattached to the wall.

Two french doors leading to a balcony view of the ocean struck Sonoma's eye. Sonoma opened one of the doors. Sonoma thought of the veranda at the mansion coming off of the event room and Rodrigo, and that certain yellow dress.

Sonoma sat down at a table and stared out over the ocean. It's dimensions were vast, its colors disparate. The ocean water was now turquoise in some areas and deep blue in others, black strips separating them, clouds playing with the water hide and seek games.

A breeze ran past Sonoma, tickling her nose.

Things were starting to make sense.

The other french door opened.

It was Max.

Max sat down solemnly.

Sonoma stared straight ahead.   Sonoma wasn't

shocked at Max's arrival. Sonoma had expected him as soon as she left the tenth floor.

"You're not real," Sonoma said to Max calmly.

Sonoma then turned her head toward Max, staring straight into his eyes.

Max was silent.

Sonoma was calm and composed. "You lied to me. You had me believe you."

Max grabbed Sonoma's arm. "Belief? Do you think that this is about belief?"

The ocean waves suddenly rose three feet then clamored over, mirroring the hostility in Max's voice.

"I can see the change, Max!" Sonoma laughed out with sarcasm. "I see how the water just changed! Isn't that what you wanted?"

Max let go of Sonoma's arm.

Sonoma didn't stop. "The mountains aren't here Max," Sonoma said harshly, turning away from Max as she stared out into the ocean. "They were here yesterday."

"You see what you want to see, Sonoma. It's that way for everyone."

"See?" Sonoma said in a disheartened tone. "See what? I don't know what is real. Is anything real? My whole life has been a lie, one great illusion-upon-illusion."

Sonoma rubbed her eyes, tears building up inside of them.

"I am real," Max said to Sonoma deliberately, with force. "I am as real as you. You and I are no different."

"Then what is going on? The mountains …the ocean…the apparitions, the sounds. It's destructive, it's assaulting, it's changing…"

"Life is never constant. Residual upon residual is how our world is built. From reincarnations of ourselves to reinventions of ourselves, is there really a difference? We are always in a state of change. But one thing's for certain: we see what we choose to see. We project into our reality by choice things that we need to see, whether we know it or not."

"You're talking gibberish at this point."

Max slammed his hand down on the table. "You're changing!" Max said. "I see it right now!"

"No I'm not. I came here to Argentina to heal. To confront my past, to leave it behind me. Instead, it follows me."

A long paused elapsed.

Sonoma stood up and looked below, seeing the sand's designs carved by the ocean's waves.

Max relaxed his tone. "Energy can't be destroyed, but its form can be changed. Just like the mountains. Just like the ocean. But you have to let it in. That's why I said that it's following you. Each spiritual fracture is a painting wanting to be seen…to be heard…to be known, to express itself fully. Once that happens, it's purpose is over. The energy is then ready to transform into a different mission."

Sonoma turned around, her focus entirely upon him. "And what about you, Max?" she said with heightened energy. "What's your story? Where did you come from? What's the true story of you that you're carrying on your back?"

Max sat back in his chair. Sonoma was challenging him directly, leaning against the rail. Sonoma's blonde hair was flying in the wind like it wanted to dislodge, escape the turmoil.

"My story is with you. That's my story. That's where I'm going, and that's where I've been. That's all I've ever wanted to be, with you."

"You were a soldier," Sonoma said softly, sitting back down.

Max smiled wide with pride, Sonoma's enhanced senses taking over.

"And you were killed. Killed in battle, in the 1800's," Sonoma continued.

Max smiled even more emphatically, enthralled at Sonoma's heightened perception.

"And you died here. Near this place. Near this ocean, where the battle took place."

The silence deepened between them.

"I found you," Max said. "It was the only battle that I've ever won, but the battle was against myself."

The ocean waves suddenly came to a stop.

"I was at Café Piraza almost a year before I died. I lived and worked there. It was housing for soldiers, like me."

"Yes, I know," Sonoma said solemnly.

"I had served three years in battle and won many awards. But I wasn't courageous. I'd wonder every day if it'd be my last. Battle after battle, killing others, war was the worst experience of my life. Twenty years old, I was a young man with a lot to learn. The best time of my life was when I lived and worked at Café Piraza before I died. I taught soldiers to read and write. I'd plan futures with them, and my future too, knowing deep down that none of us would ever have them."

"The last battle, however, got me. I died, death a term of art now, I know. I passed to a new dimension where the true arms of justice touched my soul. I was then asked to reincarnate, to learn lessons that I'd missed. They sent me into solitude, a sabbatical or sorts, to learn to forgive myself, the hardest lesson of all. I travelled worlds searching for the meaning of forgiveness. Worlds that I could not understand… Worlds in which I did not belong… I came back to Café Piraza, knowing that I'd find the answer there, the place that I loved."

Sonoma knew that it was all true.

"Then I found you. I saw you as a child and then a young lady, inflicted with trauma more severe than any battle wounds that I'd ever suffered. I cared for you, so helpless and weak. As a spirit, I co-existed with you, though you were alive in human form. I learned to communicate with you, though you did not consciously understand my language. I would sit with you on the bench and help you catch butterflies. I taught you to read in Café Piraza's library through the older children, though you couldn't hear my words. I then found you a way out of Café Piraza, through Mother Agnes, far away from Café Piraza's walls."

Sonoma was speechless.

"You didn't want to go, you know," Max said Sonoma, breaking the flurry that Sonoma felt.

"What do you mean?"

"You didn't want to leave your sisters and brother at Café Piraza. I'm the one that pushed you out. I had to, to save you. You would not have survived."

Max smiled again another wide, radiant smile. "You are ascending. I see it. Within the past few hours, you've already transitioned to a higher awareness."

Max wanted to tell Sonoma more…everything. But he couldn't. Max knew the limits that had been imposed on him which he could not exceed. Max wanted to tell Sonoma the truth about his father and Ebetrio and about the metallic bag. About Max's relations with Magda many years ago, Magda's extortion so that Max could gain information about Sonoma to try to save Sonoma. About the nights that Max would sleep alone at Café Piraza watching residuals of Sonoma as a young lady…studying them like movies. About Sonoma's energy, grace, and beauty that he saw all of the years, despite the terrorizing scenes. And about Jerusalem and William, and about his precious relationship with Aubella, and even Mother Agnes.

"I've got to confront them," Sonoma said. "The residuals need to be set free from the silt."

Max nodded in appreciation of Sonoma's words, Sonoma's senses continuing to expand.

Max rode back to Café Piraza with Sonoma in the cab. Max didn't say a word to the cab driver. Max didn't want to talk to him. Max and the cab driver knew why.

CHAPTER 31

At 3:00 a.m., Sonoma got up and looked out the bedroom window. The moon was full and bright, just like in storybooks that Sonoma had read as a child.

A giant limb from the front tree swayed eerily close to the window. The limb looked like it was waving, like it was communicating hello.

Instinctually, Sonoma walked to the foyer door. Sonoma opened the door slowly. Cool air rushed in like it had been waiting to come in, impatiently.

Sonoma touched the sign, "Café Piraza." The sign's wood was hollow, full of holes, like its heart. It's letters were written in calligraphic style, a once popular font which now only showed up on wedding invitations. The sign's gold paint was outdated too. It was crackled and chipped, deteriorated by the storms outside of Café Piraza and inside its walls. Sonoma could feel the sign's yearning to fall. Sonoma removed the sign easily. The nails that had once bound it to the door were ready to fall too.

Sonoma walked out onto the porch, leaving the door

open.

The porch wood creaked, old age. Sonoma felt splinters in the wood with her toes as she walked nimbly over the loose, shaky planks.

Sonoma sat down on the concrete steps. The evening air was soft, like the archangels on duty that night had spun it themselves with feathers of their own wings. A frog called out. A cricket chirped under the porch.

Sonoma saw a shooting star. The bright light zipped through the sky and then out of sight. Sonoma wondered about the star's family, the millions of other stars that looked to be sewn into the black fabric of the sky and seeming to whisper that they could be pulled down a different way, if one simply held their hands high enough to reach them.

Suddenly, Sonoma gasped.

A realization came over her. The days at the mansion had been almost identical.

Sonoma's realization expanded. The days before the mansion, while living in the Challengers dormitory, had essentially been the same too. The structure... The meetings... The schedules... Sonoma thought of the similarities of each day that vastly outnumbered the differences.

Sonoma then realized that her garden, "On Defining God," was no different. The garden had always been the same. The flowers had always been in bloom, irrespective of each flower's blooming period or zone.

Sonoma looked up at the stars and asked them, "Am I living in a residual? A loop of energy with structure that varies by free will?"

"Yes," a deep, dark voice answered.

Sonoma jumped up in fright.

Max stood before her. Max's face was filled with

anger and rage, a look that Sonoma had never before seen.

"Max, you scared me! I've never seen like you this!" Sonoma yelled out with confusion.

"You have, many times. You just don't remember."

Max glared at Sonoma. His eyes were black. Max looked like William. Max's voice was concrete and stoic. "I wondered how long it would take you to transide, for your understanding to fully shift. You certainly taxed my patience."

Max then laughed, expelling dark, mirthful sounds.

Sonoma was frozen in fear.

The sounds were not of Max's essence, but rather the essence of William. William's laugh was coming through Max's mouth, Sonoma knew. Max was not a stringed puppet in the moment. Max was himself, expressing the karmic sediment within him that his father had bestowed upon him, his karmic inheritance.

Suddenly, a car began driving up the sharp incline of Café Piraza. The sound hadn't been audible until that instant. It was a long, rusty green car. Loud music blared from its windows. The car then recklessly gunned forward in speed, jolting back and forth, showing its own instability that matched that of the road. Cigarette smoke poured out of the driver's window and a back window too.

As the car approached, Sonoma ran off the concrete steps in front of the house waving her hands frantically.

The car came to a rough and sudden halt. Magda got out of the car in a black, hugging dress taking a deep draw from her cigarette. "Now you guys be quiet, you hear? I do the talking," Magda instructed Angeli and Matio through the cracked, back window.

"Magda! Magda! Help me!" Sonoma screamed.

Magda was unimpressed by Sonoma, like Sonoma was not there. Magda started walking toward the concrete steps.

Max laughed. "She doesn't see you Sonoma," Max said poignantly.

"Magda! I'm here!" Sonoma yelled.

Again, Magda was unphased.

"Don't you get it?" Max chided. "Only you see her. She can't see you."

Sonoma followed Magda up the concrete steps and onto the porch. Sonoma moved her arms through Magda's body, feeling only cool air.

Magda knocked loudly on the door. Magda then engaged in dialogue with a man's voice, the man invisible.

Sonoma recognized Max's voice.

Sonoma watched the residual energy play. Max watched too, the scene unfolding almost exactly as it did days before. Sonoma shuttered upon learning of Magda's nights with Max and Max's study of Sonoma, and extortion. Sonoma watched Magda assault Max and then speed off in the car, stripping gears as Magda plummeted the drive with fearful rage then disappearing before she reached the incline leading to the road.

"Did you kill her? Did you hurt her?" Sonoma screamed at Max.

"No. Never. I would never hurt her. It is Magda's spiritual fracture playing out, not mine."

"I need to know what happened to Magda here to cause this residual!"

"It's not your story. It's not your projection."

Sonoma dropped to the ground. Adrenalin had stopped the fight, sending Sonoma's body into numbness, a self-encapsulating state. Sonoma could not speak or move.

Thirty minutes elapsed. Max nervously waited for the right and left sides of Sonoma's brain to reunite so that Sonoma could function again.

"I have been living in a residual of my own, haven't I?"

Max walked over and sat down next to Sonoma. "You have."

"My books have had the same themes. My events have been the same, even the guests. My schedule has been mostly the same for years."

"You've been living in loops. We all live in them."

Sonoma sat up, alert and took a deep breath. "What about Aubella? Is she a residual too?" Sonoma cupped her face with her hands, afraid of the answer.

"Does it matter? Does it truly matter if Aubella is what you call 'real' or not?" Max asked.

"It matters, Max! She is my child. You love her too."

"Aubella is real, Sonoma," Max said, calming his tone. "So are you."

"I want the loops to stop."

Sonoma rose and sat on the bench.

More time elapsed.

"None of us are real, are we?" Sonoma asked bluntly, with edge.

"It depends on what you call 'real.'"

Max stood and walked over to the bench. Sonoma looked up at him, her eyes silently approving him to sit.

Max sat down and reached for Sonoma's hand. "You just did it. You changed your perception."

Max's eyes were now blue and his hair solid black, no silver speckles in its midst. Max felt the warmth of Sonoma's hand, bringing Max back to what he called reality. "Sonoma… We all live in residuals in some way. How many times do we replay events in our heads when we're driving down the road? How many times do we repeat behavior, over and over, allowing history to repeat itself right before our eyes? How many times do we teach children behaviors, traits, embedded with us, to see them play out again and again? And karma is a loop of its own breed, full of reoccurring patterns which we can create, inherit, take, and give. We live and we die. We live and we die, the ultimate loop."

"We see what we want to see," Sonoma said in a low voice.

"That is the power of intention. How you focus your perception determines your life. Give yourself permission to see things differently and you'll find yourself transforming mountains into an ocean. It is the essence of miracles."

"Miracles…," Sonoma said, then looking back up at the stars. "I have seen miracles."

Max was silent.

"A miracle is like looking in a mirror," Sonoma continued. "Perhaps that's where the word comes from. I face it, and it faces me. We stare at each other endlessly in a war of reflection. We're both the hunter and the hunted. In the persistence of my stare, I lose my focus. I start to see through my assailant's eyes staring at me, looking at myself. The war then ends."

Sonoma's transition was complete.

CHAPTER 32

Sonoma slept more soundly that night, despite the few remaining hours, than she had ever slept before.

The mathematical equation had finally presented itself, the equation that could never be solved and wasn't designed to be solved but only expressed. There was no winner. There was no loser. Only expression, the essence of love.

Sonoma remembered Dr. Stark at the chalkboard on her first day of school at the Challengers Foundation. Dr. Stark had written parts of the equation on the board that day, but the concepts had been foreign to her.

Stretching and yawning, Sonoma turned and kissed Max gently on his cheek. Max was still asleep. Sonoma could smell Max's white t-shirt bearing his essence mixed with cologne.

Sonoma studied Max's black hair, his perfect nose, and masculine shoulders. Max smiled, feeling Sonoma's eyes upon him. "Such beauty," Max joked.

"We're similar creatures," Max said to Sonoma,

smiling.

"You say that all the time... But we are," Sonoma said back, kissing Max's shoulders softly and then his cheeks and lips.

Max loved Sonoma with all of his soul, with all of his life, with every ounce of his being. Magnetism brought and bound them together.

"I want a baby," Sonoma whispered, "...a brother or sister for Aubella."

Max turned to Sonoma ferociously, holding her tightly up against him.

Sonoma didn't stop. "I want to build residuals within residuals."

And the sediment being fertile, the two made love passionately in the morning. There were no flying chandeliers. No residual interruptions. No uninvited voices. Only the sound of their lovemaking as the morning sun enveloped them and the shadows disappeared.

CHAPTER 33

Sonoma walked through the garden doorway and touched the sign "On Defining God," joyous to be back. Sonoma was fresh off the plane, having arrived back to the mansion mid-morning, only minutes ago. The flowers released honey and citrus wood scents as soon as Sonoma entered, delighted that she was back. The garden was healthy and vibrant, just like it had always been. Sonoma felt healthy and vibrant too as she surveyed the paradise around her, glad to be back in Miami after two weeks in Argentina.

Sonoma walked the entire garden, greeting each flower one-by-one. Sonoma touched the green stalk of a peach peony, feeling soft fuzz on its stalk. Then a red rose, its pedals being tightly wound and compressed, not ready to open, sleeping in late. Then a sunflower, the most cheerful flower of all. Sonoma eyed its long stalk, five feet high, touching its giant circle bloom, admiring its large size and compared to its docile spirit.

Sonoma then noticed green ivy growing like crazed tentacles up a brick wall. It was a new occurrence for the garden, something that had never happened before. The top arms of the ivy spread and overlapped each other forming multiple green grids. In the center of the grids, red and orange flowers were blooming in clusters. Some of the flowers contained red and orange ribbon marks and splotches. Others were solid in color. All bloomed together snuggly fit within the grid, the flowers' walls, as if they were riding a magic carpet. Sonoma thought that the blooms' texture was uncanny.

"That's it!" Sonoma said.

The breed was new to Sonoma's garden. Sonoma knew every inch of her garden, every flower and plant that lived in the kingdom. The orange and red flowers were the same breed that Sonoma had seen at The Inn.

Sonoma got a ladder and climbed to the top rung to get a closer look. Sonoma wondered how the flowers had gotten into her garden, baffled at the sight. The blooming flowers looked like they had been nesting and growing for months. The blooms were mature and well connected to the ivy that bore them.

Sonoma looked down.

Ivy had entangled the ladder that was holding Sonoma in the air.

Sonoma tilted back on the ladder, as if to fall.

The wound ivy held the ladder in place. It was like the ivy had grown and encircled the ladder within the few seconds that Sonoma had been standing on it.

Sonoma looked back up at the flowers and then onto the ceiling.

"What is this?" Sonoma said. Sonoma saw a cut-out in the ceiling. "Is this an attic?"

Sonoma climbed down and got a broom. Sonoma then climbed back up the ladder and used the broom to push on the ceiling cut-out. It resisted her push.

Sonoma pushed again.

The ceiling square dropped. A ladder popped out in front of Sonoma like a genie in a bottle.

"Strange," Sonoma said, studying the ladder dangling before her.

Sonoma then used the broom to elongate the attic ladder.

Finally stretched out from the ground to the ceiling cut-out, Sonoma then descended the ivy ladder and climbed onto the attic ladder. Sonoma climbed the stairway of rungs quickly, reaching the top, emerging view with ease.

Sonoma looked at the vast space of the attic, baffled at the sight. Sonoma then climbed into the space, like a vacuum inhaled her.

Sonoma was amazed. The space, which was hidden over the garden, was over two thousand square feet. It had tall ceilings, almost twelve feet in height from the attic floor. The space had a fully furnished den, kitchen, dining room, and bedroom. The rooms were spotlessly clean and contained modern appliances.

"On Defining God, you have mysteries within you," Sonoma said to the space.

Sonoma then noticed a separating wall behind the den. Sonoma walked behind it, still exploring the space. There was a long, narrow hallway of ten rooms. Each room had a door that was numbered, consecutively ranging from 1-10.

Sonoma walked to door no. 1. Sonoma tried to open the door, but it was locked.

Sonoma walked to door no. 2. It was also locked.

All of the doors were locked, or so it seemed. However, when Sonoma walked to door no. 10, the door opened.

Sonoma walked inside cautiously.

On the floor, in the center of the small room, was an old, dilapidated chandelier. Sonoma recognized it immediately. It was the old chandelier from Café Piraza that had hung in the kitchen for decades until the decorators had recently removed it, replacing it with a modern but repeatedly crashing and regenerating chandelier.

Sonoma felt sadness come over here, despondent energy in the room.

Sonoma noticed a closet. Sonoma opened the closet doors. The closet was almost as large as the room. There was a bag on the floor in the center of the closet.

Sonoma reached for the bag. A wave of confusion came over Sonoma and which flooded Sonoma's nervous system, causing Sonoma's equilibrium to craze. Sonoma lost her balance, falling into the closet on the floor.

Sonoma's face landed in the rippled folds of a large, shiny metallic bag.

CHAPTER 34

By late mid-morning, Max was at the Challengers Foundation meeting with staff.

During the staff meeting, Max began to feel ill. Within ten minutes, Max was gravely ill, experiencing acute flu symptoms and throbbing pains in his head. Sweat rolled off Max's face. Max's body was drenched in sweat underneath his clothes. Max's balance was impaired such that he didn't know if he could walk. Max knew with a certainty that something was severely wrong.

Max quickly excused himself from the meeting and ran for the bathroom, barely making it into a stall.

Max fell face first into the toilet seat, vomiting violently.

"Are you okay, Mr. McCallister?" a female assistant yelled to Max from the bathroom door.

Max couldn't respond.

Max finished and wiped his mouth, then locked the door. Max couldn't speak. Max could barely walk. It was like a fog of dementia filled him.

The female assistant heard the latch lock. She walked

away.

Max looked into the mirror. His eyes were darkening and turning black. Max's hair was speckled gray, no longer solid black. Max looked just like William.

Max got closer to the mirror, staring straight into his own eyes.

One minute passed.

Max saw all that he needed to see.

"Oh my God!" Max screamed, pounding his fists into the glass repeatedly.

The glass didn't shatter, but parts of Max did.

CHAPTER 35

The unwrapped white tissue paper on the closet floor looked like freshly fallen snow. The crisp paper was ruffled and tethered, and torn in places, but still expressed the qualities of peace and truth that it embodied and shrouded.

The bag lay empty on the floor. Its inside belly was twisted and pulled out, like its organs had been removed. The paper's job of concealing was finally over.

Sonoma sat quietly looking at the unwrapped items before her. Some of the items still had tape strapped to their backs from the connecting tissue paper, like they were saddles of unruly horses, their riders flung. Sonoma was paralyzed in shock. The shock was a buffer. To protect Sonoma, a type of energetic coma to protect the landscape of her mind. Sonoma was holding onto a lock of baby blonde hair attached to an ivory-embossed card with Aubella's name and the words "2 years old" written on it. A picture of William and Aubella, along with Mother Agnes and Max, was clipped to it. They were smiling in the picture at a birthday party, for Aubella, two years old. The Challengers building in Jerusalem was in the background.

There were no tears or shrieks from Sonoma. There were no cries. There was only acknowledgment, forced recognition of the reality that the items contained.

Sonoma heard someone walking down the hallway, their pace fast. Sonoma didn't recognize the source of the patterned, spirited steps.

"How could you!" Max yelled while brashly entering the room. "I saved your life! And you do this to me?" Max exclaimed.

Sonoma was unphased. No words emanated from her lips. Sonoma did not move.

Max grabbed Sonoma's legs from the closet and pulled her out into the center of the room. "Talk to me!" he yelled.

Sonoma stared up at Max, who was towering above her. Max face was William's face, drenched in anger and rage.

Max kicked the chandelier with forceful might. Broken chandelier parts flew across and around the room.

Sonoma then heard more footsteps, not recognizing the quickening pace of them either.

Dr. Stark entered. "Max! I'm sorry," Dr. Stark said with deliberation. "I'll get this taken care of."

Dr. Stark then knelt down to Sonoma, putting his hand on her cheek. "She feels cold, Max," Dr. Stark said.

Dr. Stark then pulled out a needle. "You're going to be okay, Sonoma. Just stay with me. Everything will be okay."

CHAPTER 36

Sonoma could hear voices coming in and out. The voices were sometimes near, while others were far away. Male voices. Female voices. They were coming from all directions. Sonoma kept her eyes shut all the while.

"Dr. Stark...," a female voice said. Sonoma couldn't hear the rest of the female's words.

Suddenly, Sonoma saw herself at five years old in her mind's eye. The child was her playing on the bench at Café Piraza with a doll.

Then suddenly, Sonoma was nine years old. It was in the evening, after dinner. Sonoma was in the library at Café Piraza teaching younger children alphabet letters.

Then a knock on the door sounded.

"Sonoma, it's time," a man said with a deep voice, gristling through the door.

Sonoma saw herself leave the library. Sonoma then saw herself standing in the middle of a line of seven young girls. There was a window in the middle of the room. Sonoma could see a shiny, black car outside the window. There was movement. The car door opened. Three men got out of the car and walked inside, opening the door with familiarity.

Three men walked down the line of seven girls, groping them fervently with their eyes. Sonoma recognized one of them. It was William, Max's father. William pointed to Sonoma.

Sonoma could then hear herself breathing. Taking breaths… Inhaling and exhaling… Sonoma could hear her heart beating too, though each beat had no reverence or cognizance of what was happening to her, what he was doing to her.

Sonoma was alive. That's all that mattered, Sonoma thought to herself, waiting for it to be over. It will be over soon, Sonoma thought. The faces of the other two men who had gotten out of the car flashed in Sonoma's mind. Sonoma remembered. They had selected her before…from the same line…many times. One man wore a freshly pressed striped suit. The man wore it to every session. The other man wore a gold coin necklace, shiny and bright, and his words were always few, if any.

Then the scene went black. Sonoma felt dizzy and unbalanced. Like Sonoma was in between dreams, jumping back and forth from and into private worlds which were no longer private but showing to Sonoma.

Sonoma opened her eyes.

CHAPTER 37

Sonoma awoke to find herself lying in bed. Sonoma's head and body were bolstered with pillows. The bed was assembled in the same room in which Sonoma had collapsed, room no. 10.

Four chairs were placed around the bed. Dr. Stark was sitting in the chair closest to Sonoma, covering his face with his hands.

Sonoma sat up slowly.

"Where is everyone else?" Sonoma asked.

"Thank God you're awake," Dr. Stark said with sincerity and concern, looking up.

"How long have I been asleep?"

"Almost twenty-four hours."

"Where is Max?"

"He's at the foundation. He went there to review groupings, to try to find a cure."

"A cure...," Sonoma said, confused.

"A cure for you."

Sonoma paused.

"What happened to me?"

"You walked into Max's laboratory. Max studies groupings and residual energy there. That's why the old chandelier was in the room, so that Max could study its energy."

"But why did it hurt me? Why did it send me into a place of confusion?"

"You saw a 'residual implant.' It's when a material item having residual energy is moved to a new location. When the move occurs, the item has to acclimate to its new environment…grow new roots, if you will. The old chandelier hadn't been in this room but only a few days, after being shipped from Argentina recently. One of the crews must have forgotten to lock the door. When you came in, because the chandelier contains trauma embedded in it from you, you then felt what it felt, mass confusion. This is uncharted data, unstudied territory, what happened to you. Max discovered that you had entered the tenth room when he experienced violent reality shifts because of his connection to you, his grouping with you. Max was feeling what you were feeling. Groupings are like two balloons flying together and feeling the same stimuli so that one can help the other grow."

Max walked in.

"She's awake Max," Dr. Stark said.

Max released a resounding sigh of relief. "Praise God."

Dr. Stark left the room to give Sonoma and Max privacy.

"I'm so glad that you are okay," Max said. "I've been searching for any type of possible cure. This is uncharted territory, what happened to you yesterday."

"That's what Dr. Stark said."

"I've been worried sick," Max said.

Sonoma's voice got stronger. "You've been worried because I finally found out who you are....what you are, and what you've been doing to me all these years."

"What are you talking about," Max said in disgust, shaking his head.

"You've been studying me. That's been your purpose the whole time. Perhaps I should now study you."

Sonoma rose from the bed and walked out of the room.

Max followed behind her.

Sonoma walked down the short hallway and stopped in front of door number 1.

"The attic...," Sonoma turned and said to Max. "Attachments... Nice pun, Max." Sonoma then turned the doorknob. The door opened with ease.

The room was dark, almost black. An orb of light hovered in the center of the room.

In the orb was a scene of a fallen male soldier. He was lying motionless in the battlefield. His eyes were open. He could hear. He could see. His clothes were soaked in blood. The soldier was aware that he was dying.

Two chairs were in the room, not far from the hovering orb. Sonoma sat down, as did Max, like they had been commanded to sit. The door shut slowly on its own.

A swirl of energy from the orb then began spiraling and then stretching and elongating. It then expanded, turning into what appeared to be a movie screen with blurred edges on its sides.

The movie began.

Sonoma saw Café Piraza being built. Sonoma could feel the high hopes of the builders. Government officials were banded together at the site laying the first rocks of what they had said would be the town's salvation.

Sonoma could feel no darkness in the hands that laid the rocks, only hope for a better tomorrow and today and for all to live in harmony. Then Sonoma could see soldiers living and working in Café Piraza, some living there before going to war and others after returning from it. The screen focused on a young man who was teaching other soldiers in a small room.

Then the scene changed. Sonoma saw that same young man as a soldier dying in a field, matching the impression in the orb when Sonoma first entered. The young man had been shot in the chest. Other men were falling down next to him, shot too...dying too. Sonoma could feel the young man's energy. The young man was Max though his face was not the same as Sonoma knew it.

"It is you," Sonoma said to Max. "Just like I told you at The Inn."

Max nodded.

Then the movie changed. With another swirl, the scene was changed to Café Piraza. Sonoma saw Café Piraza after the war, after Max died. The scene showed the young man still sitting in the small room waiting for a soldier student, but no more soldiers were coming to learn.

Then children's voices were audible. Then Sonoma saw the sign "Café Piraza" being put on the front door. Fresh paint... Fresh writing... Café Piraza's reign of terror commenced. Then screams of agony and beatings sounded as Sonoma saw government officials lining up to go into the many rooms, rooms in which she had been a fixture.

Then Sonoma saw herself again as a child. Sonoma was in the library. Older students were teaching her to read. Max was sitting next to Sonoma, though her human eyes didn't see him. Max was teaching Sonoma to read in a silent language that Sonoma understood but could not acknowledge in human language.

"I felt you. I felt you then," Sonoma said to Max with excitement and gratitude at the vision.

"Yes, you did," Max said with a wide smile. "You did... You saw me with your inner eyes. And I saw you."

Then the movie slowly ended like a candle suffocating, its wick finally having run its course, its mission complete.

"Sonoma, we all have rooms that we carry with us. Some rooms are locked. Some are open. Some have contents that continually drip and we leave trails of it wherever we go."

"Residual energy," Sonoma said succinctly.

"Yes."

"You died in the war. You were at Café Piraza before you left, but then you came back."

"I loved Café Piraza. Café Piraza was good to me. It helped me and so many other soldiers before the war. I was poor. I had no place to go. I had no home. Café Piraza gave me a home and a place to share with other soldiers."

"Where did you go when you died?"

Max laughed. "When I passed?"

"Yes."

"I went to be judged. Not by others, but myself. Jesus Christ and his council were at my side supporting me. I judged myself harshly. I then decided to go back, to learn how to correct my failings. That's when I found you."

Sonoma was quiet.

"I found you in the library. I watched you grow. I studied you. I saw the torture that you suffered. Every day, I prayed for a way to help you and the other children at Café Piraza. I petitioned the councils hundreds fold to help you. I then found a way…a way to get you out of Café Piraza through Mother Agnes, my saintly mother. But I had to use your residual energy which attracted me to you in the first place."

"You had to use evil," Sonoma abruptly interjected.

"I had to use what you call evil, expression of that energy."

"And so I allowed myself to be birthed as William's son, William being the second in command to Ebetrio. William was Ebetrio's brother. It was the only way that I could reach you, to be woven into your life. Mother Agnes allowed herself to manifest on this plane, to perform mission work with William."

"But what about time? You were birthed when I was a child? How could you be older than I am?"

"There is no such thing as time, only perception…perception of time."

The moment summoned Sonoma. Sonoma held her hands over her eyes. "Ebetrio is the father of Aubella, Max," Sonoma said in quiet desperation.

"No, Sonoma. I am."

CHAPTER 38

Sonoma heard Max's words but couldn't process them. Sonoma played the words again in her mind, trying to absorb the meaning.

"What are you saying!" Sonoma yelled. "Are you crazy?"

Max sat in the chair quietly, wringing his hands in his lap.

"It was me that impregnated you. It was me that bound you. It was me that loved you. I was it all. I overtook every man that would line up and enter your room as much as I could, to save you. I channeled my energy through them, to eradicate as much of their energy as I could. It was the only way that I could save your life. They would have killed you, just like they did many other children."

"I should kill you for what you did to me! You are just like your father. You dabble in good and evil, whichever serves you better at the time. And maybe good is slightly weighted more on your shoulder than evil on the other, but you're still vile. You are a monster that kills but then brings flowers to the grave. Maybe I should take the knife that was in your father's bag and use it on you! The one that William gave Gilda to kill Ebetrio with after Gilda started the Mt. Ezeria fire!"

"How could you say that? William was trying to eradicate the bad!"

"Well he failed. Your father utterly failed. He failed miserably. I hope that he takes his failure with him when he someday makes his rise."

"William is dead."

"William is not dead!"

"You are delusional, Sonoma!"

"Really? Then let's go to the next room and open up the door… And then to the next, until all of the doors are wide open. Shall we?"

"You are crazy! This is my laboratory!"

"This is your collection of residuals! Your own prison!" Sonoma yelled.

Sonoma ran out of the room and kicked the door open to room number 2.

"No!" Max screamed, grabbing Sonoma's neck.

Hundreds of purple doves flew out of the room, swooping and sweeping, like their wings were stretching and soaring for the first time in decades. The splendor grabbed the moment more than the pressure around Sonoma's neck. Sonoma flung Max off of her and onto the floor. The strength that Sonoma felt within her was an imminence that finally made its presence known.

Sonoma then kicked all of the other doors open. A young man looking like Dr. Stark came running out into the hallway. So did Magda, Matio, and Angeli, having finally broken free from the locked door that had been imprisoning them. Other people poured out into the hallway too, and including the nameless patron from the diner in the striped suit, whom Sonoma immediately recognized in all of his dimensions, as well as the cab driver wearing his gold coin necklace. They were standing in the hallway celebrating that the door had finally opened, that they had finally been set free.

Then suddenly, they quieted.

Silence prefaced another shift coming.

Room number 9 was about to become empty. Its doors glided open as though it were revolving… Around an invisible curvature, path, then circling back around.

It was William. William was in the room. Max was in the room too, standing next to him. They were facing the open door with solace in their eyes, the face of karma unzipped.

Across from them in the room, chained to the wall, was Rodrigo, dressed in formal military attire. Rodrigo had been Max's opponent, the one who had shot the fatal bullet that pierced Max's chest, killing Max on the battlefield.

Rodrigo's chains fell from his hands, slamming to the ground.

Rodrigo then began removing his pins and accolades, his fine shirted collection, all of them… His badges of courage that were now remnants of pain, having finally expressed their course. Rodrigo was placing them in a box, to heat, to change the pins' metals into liquid, to fill a new mold.

Mother Agnes then appeared in the hallway, who looked sixteen years old. William ran out into the hallway and embraced her, and she him. All the while, Sonoma and Max watched, distanced but near, as the melt began.

The hallway erupted with commemoration, flooding the hall with graduation of awareness. The feeling that flowers feel when they finally realize that stifling weeds had been their allies all along and that their enemies-in-disguise had sheltered them in higher realms' ways, weeds being the most beautiful flowers of all.

Each person had made their presence known. Each person had acknowledged the presence of each other. Their individual but collective expression, heaven's study, was complete. The unsolvable equation had been expressed.

Then the lights went dark. A new screen. Now blank. A new unexpressed equation presenting itself... Only Max and Sonoma were standing in front of the hallway, now empty.

They had all disappeared.

CHAPTER 39

"There are residuals all around us," Sonoma typed.

"Residuals of ourselves, of others, of trauma, of pain, which we carry with us everywhere that we go."

Sonoma reflected on the words which manifested like heavy, falling rain.

"We must give ourselves permission to change our perception, the kaleidoscope that is ingrained within us. Kick the doors to the residual energies open and require them to express. Hidden trap doors no more... We then become conductors of our own projected music, the carefully chosen notes and meters which our reality sings."

Sonoma had been writing for three hours, her next book which finally had a different theme.

Sonoma stood.

"Are you coming?" Max said to Sonoma, beckoning Sonoma to go out the door with him. "We don't want to miss the eclipse."

"Yeah mom," said little William with glee, Sonoma

and Max's five year old son.   "Aubella is at the Challengers in Argentina waiting for it too!"   Little William and Max ran out the door, their steps almost in unison.

Sonoma sat back down, staring at her computer screen.

The old sign "Café Piraza" hung above her, affixed to the wall. It had been tamed by the same roaring lions who had made the engravements, transforming its thick mountain ridges into oars of an ocean, now propelling away.   Forming new designs...   New expressions... Fresh budding flowers in the darkness born by trauma and pain, enjoying fresh light.

Forgiveness by expression had brought them together, she and the sign...the sign making its way to Sonoma after Café Piraza collapsed one uneventful Sunday afternoon two years prior. The building had passed on its own, despite the endless crews of staff that had repaired and redecorated it trying to change its essence which was temporary at best. The building had been ready to move on, pass...inhabit another form. It had expressed itself too and was ready to graduate, which it did, disappearing into the welcoming pasture that Sonoma knew would love and cherish it.

The Challengers Foundation rebuilt on Café Piraza's hallow ground, but without horizontal wings.   The building had vertical wings.   The building was thirty stories high, each floor an attic in which to examine the energetic items that made its way there, to that special place that the Challengers Foundation served - humanity - to contextually show that we can rescue each other by rescuing ourselves.   Aubella was the director of the Challengers Foundation's Argentinean mission.   The building was named "Attica de Mother Agnes."

And as the Miami air flowed through Sonoma's window that late eve, Sonoma felt something wildly new brewing.

Some new strain…

Some new breed…

Perhaps new textured flowers popping up in the kingdom, which Sonoma would find if not in a little while, then in an eternity away. By looking in the mirror for miracles, its magic starting to become commonplace.

Sonoma had resolved to find Ebetrio, who hadn't walked the hallway above the garden. Sonoma had let the wind masters know. Sonoma had fueled her resolution with intention, fearing him no more. The patterns were coming… Making their presence known…

Sonoma heard loud honks coming from outside.

"I'm coming!" Sonoma yelled through the open window, the crisp air refilling her lungs, her lungs of the sea.

Sonoma shut her computer, ready to see new designs in the sky, like a sea turtle having propelled by its mark, ready to move to the next mission.

ABOUT THE AUTHOR

After a real, wide-awake metaphysical vision and encounter with Jesus Christ on June 12, 2008, Leslie Dean Drury knew that she had to start doing what she was born to do: write. At whatever cost, wherever it took her. Fully realize the yearning to write which Leslie had felt since a child. Born in Harrodsburg, Kentucky, Leslie grew up on a small farm in a Mercer county, a rural community. In 1998, Leslie began practicing law, following her father's and other family members' footsteps by becoming an attorney. After June 12, 2008, however, Leslie's world changed, Leslie to never be the same.

"The June 12th experience was like I was being called on the carpet, and in more ways than one. I was being told that I wasn't doing my work in this life. And to just jump on, do it. Jump on the magic carpet which we all have supporting us and fly. Do what I'm born to do, fulfill my mission that I'd been ignoring since a child but knew every day without a doubt was there in my soul. I hearing its yearning voice everyday but ignoring it like so many of us do."

In 2012, Leslie moved to Naples, Florida with her husband, Melvin, and children, Aliona and Melvin II, to fully immerse herself in her journey of writing, the first book titled *Fractured*. The book's mission is aligned with that of Rasa Publishing: to embrace life deeply and with meaning, bookmark your life with joy right now, bask in the beauty of the glorious present moment.

www.ingramcontent.com/pod-product-compliance
Lightning Source LLC
Chambersburg PA
CBHW050733180626
46814CB00002B/740